AN ISRAELI LOVE STORY

AN ISRAELI LOVE STORY

ZOLA LEVITT

An Israeli Love Story

Library of Congress Cataloging in Publication Data

Levitt, Zola.
  An Israeli love story.

  I. Title.
  PZ4.L6664Is   [PS3562.E9226]   813'.5'4   77-27611

ISBN: 978-0-802441-81-2 Print edition
ISBN: 978-1-930749-40-5 eBook edition

ONE

Isaac was pinned down. He dared not move.

The Palestinian on the roof across the walk-way was a marksman, that much was sure. It would be pure insanity for Isaac or any of the others to show themselves.

No one had been hit so far by the bursts of rifle fire from behind the ledge, but that was only because they had all taken cover from the terrorist. Word on the walkie-talkie from the kibbutz border had it that this one was not to be trifled with. He had slipped through the border defenses like a ghost, giving pinpoint cover fire to his fellow terrorists, all of whom had now been killed, and he had made it on his own to his present position, directly across from the nursery. He held a flat roof with raised eaves.

The sniper had to be eliminated. But how?

Isaac fought within himself while deciding what action would be necessary if the Palestin-ian tried to attack the nursery with rifle fire. He resolved to show himself and draw the fire. He would shoot it out with the demon while

5

the others moved up. In no case could this miserable terrorist be allowed to fire on the defenseless nursery.

The terrorist probably did not know the nursery was within his range. Possibly he was enough of a human being not to attack little children, but this philosophy could not be trusted. Terrorists came to accomplish terror—to horrify the enemy with their utter disregard for life, their own or others'. The nursery was an unmarked building—a house like any other on the kibbutz. At that early hour the children were still inside, and no toys were in the yard yet. Perhaps the intruder did not realize that the impassive building, completely silent because of the drills the children had been taught for just such moments, was in fact so vulnerable. Perhaps he preferred to remain where he was without revealing his position, thinking that the Israelis had failed to trace his movements through the main compound.

Isaac was exhausted from his long morning in the fields. It was now about nine a.m., but work had started at four because of the hot season. Isaac had been due a break for rest in the later morning and afternoon before he went back out into the blistering rows of crops at four that afternoon. He was tired, and he was not prepared for this—fighting with a desperate, suicidal rifleman of consummate skill and deadly resolve. Isaac would rather have been anywhere on the earth than crouched behind the strange metal sculpture that graced the walkway in front of the nursery.

The sculpture was grey steel, with red rocket-casings welded to it in some kind of abstract statement of Israeli power. It was meant to defy the world, Isaac thought, rather than to provide skimpy cover for a farmer with a rifle in hand. It was never meant as a defense against these creatures straight from hell, who came in the night and shot women and children, blew up buildings, and hunted down innocents.

Sweat ran through his curled black beard and dripped to the ground in front of his flushed face. His deeply tanned forehead was lined in concentration; to look away even for an instant and allow the sniper to possibly take a new angle on his position could be fatal. Isaac knew exactly where the Palestinian was on the roof, just as the Palestinian knew exactly where Isaac was behind the steel structure. Isaac realized his adversary would stop at nothing to make a kill; there was no way out for him now, anyway. At this point, the Palestinian would serve his miserable cause best by taking as many Israelis as possible to the grave with him.

There was total, eerie silence as the stalemate progressed.

Then, barely audibly, Isaac's walkie-talkie

began to whisper. He had it braced directly against his ear. He heard distinctly two short, sharp barks: "Down. Grenade!"

No! Isaac's mind screamed to him as he literally ground his face into the hot sand. "Oh, God. God!" he whispered. He was barely fifty feet from the terrorist. Someone was going to try to hit the roof with a hand grenade. There would be shrapnel, an explosion. *My God! My God!* Isaac cried within himself.

He wanted to have courage; he wanted to be still, to concentrate, to be ready to move immediately if the sniper tried to jump to the walkway. But he was frozen in terror, knowing only that his body—plain, soft flesh—was stretched out on the ground within easy range of hundreds of bits of hurtling sharp metal. The grenade could miss the roof; it could land beside him. He didn't know the position of the grenade thrower, or whether he was a soldier at all. Perhaps he was the only man within range. Perhaps he was an old man with a trembling arm. Perhaps he was as terrified as Isaac, and unable to hurl the lethal missile accurately.

Isaac had always been cynical of war movies and the phony, staged dramas of television. There the fighters ran at tanks, covered grenades with their bodies, laughed as they routed the enemy. It made good entertainment, but in the moment when one's own arms and legs were out there for the butchering—when the issue was whether one might survive or be torn to pieces in an instant—then fear, cold, nauseating, selfish fear, completely took over. There passed through Isaac's panicky brain the clear knowledge that he would have sacrificed the nursery itself for his own safety. *Take all the children, and do what you want! Let me live another day!*

No. Isaac rejected that thought. He knew himself a little better than that. He was no Israeli hero to be read about and admired the world over. He was no Entebbe commando. But he had always manned his post, and he had always defended his people. He was quiet, bookish, concerned with life and death in a more spiritual way than with bullets and fire. But when Israel needed his help, such as it was, he had always been ready.

Isaac felt comforted in those moments as he waited for the terrible explosion to occur so near to where he lay. He knew he would be ready for whatever came next. His finger was on the trigger of his rifle—he dared not remove his hands from his weapon to hold his ears—and his legs were warm and twitching. Knowing that his body would serve him in a moment, in whatever would be required of it, he seemed to get a second wind of courage.

Inside the nursery Rebecca sat calmly facing the door. She was in the front room, about twenty feet from the doorway. Her gaze was level, her mouth dry and tight. She was absolutely motionless. An Uzi submachine gun lay across her knees.

She felt little fear, only a kind of loathing. Fully expecting the door to burst open, she was ready to fill the front of the room with machine gun fire. She had practiced this drill, and she had mastered her feelings about it. Unless she got a walkie-talkie signal first, she would blast to pieces any man coming through that doorway. If no voice came on the speaker before the door opened, or if there was gunfire outside the nursery when it opened, Rebecca would hold her gun steadily on the door and fire until the gun was too hot to cling to any longer. Then, if she were still alive, she would pause only a second before firing a second burst of the same length. She would fire her machine gun at that doorway until she died.

The children were gathered in the back room with the little cots and toy boxes. They also understood their assignment. They were deathly quiet. The oldest among them, four and five years old, played silent games with the infants. They were ready to silence any crying with a stiff hand over a baby's mouth, and ready to hang on all day if necessary. They had fully understood the instructions: "Men might come in and kill you if they hear any sound from you." They knew their assignment.

In the front room, Rebecca's gaze was murderous. If the terrorist could see the fatal glare in those otherwise deep and beautiful eyes, he would think twice about assaulting her territory. Accustomed more to warding off romantic advances of young men than of terrorists, Rebecca was still equal to her task of the moment. She had been chosen for her work partly with her supposed fighting skills in mind. Although she had never been a soldier, she was calm, intelligent, and efficient under pressure. That she was patient with children was a secondary point. That she could, and would, kill human beings with a machine gun when necessary, had been detected by the kibbutz *masker*, and this was her main qualification.

Actually, they really didn't know her all that well, because inside her woman's mind she was in no way a killer.

Rebecca did not hate men, and her prime interest in life was not really the defense of her country. She was completely bent toward love—the real kind of love, warm and true, washing over from a tender and trusting couple to their children. She was fascinated with men, how they acted, how fearfully strong and inexplicable they were. But she had never known a man intimately. Although she was in her early twenties, she had never experienced the kind of all-out love she instinctively knew was possible.

Rebecca had a certain beauty of face and body that attracted all sorts of cajoling characters who appeared in the guise of men, but they invariably repulsed her. Her face would be called haunting before it would be called pretty, and her slender, artful body seemed too delicate for a man's embrace. Her eyes penetrated and then looked away quickly, always raising men's interest.

At certain times in her teen years she had been tempted to give herself completely to a man just because he wanted her, but she knew that would be insulting to the future man for whom she had been made. Somewhere in the world there was a man who would look at her one day, and she would know that he was her man. He would know what to say, what to do. He would know Rebecca instantly, because she was his woman, made for him. She would be one flesh with him, as the Scriptures told her, and he would find her in God's time. She ached for him. For so long now she had wanted him to come.

But inside this empty heart that waited so patiently for God's man was also the resolve to watch for other men with different missions. And so, if the circumstances warranted it, she would be ready to kill the man who came through that door, and the man behind him, and the man after that.

And if she had to kill those men—and she had never harmed anyone in her life—she would be sorry, and she would be guilty, she knew. But *her* man, who would come someday, would make the memory fade, and he would know what to say to bring her back to what she really was at heart—a woman, a lover, a mother.

TWO

With every muscle clenched and his teeth grinding, Isaac thought he had prepared himself for the grenade blast, but no one could have been ready for that horrifying moment. He clutched his rifle, squeezing it as if it might deliver him from his inner confusion and terror, but his body seemed to be blown inside out by the cracking, thundering crash of the missile exploding over his head on the roof across the walkway.

As fragments of roof tile fell all around him, and bits of shrapnel dug into the ground in front of him, Isaac realized he had been spared. The grenade had landed directly on the roof, thank God, and the eaves on his side had protected him from the explosion's direct force.

It seemed as if debris was landing all around him for a long time. Some of it had been blown high into the air above the roof. But Isaac, lying perfectly still with his face crushed into the dirt, felt nothing touch him. In fact, he felt nothing at all; he suddenly realized that he was numb from head to toe.

Blinking his eyes and moving his head slowly, Isaac raised his eyes with difficulty toward the roof. He felt his blood beginning to circulate again and he realized that all of his body was still with him. He was unhurt. A glance down at his legs showed that he had escaped injury; everything was the same as before the grenade exploded, except for the litter all around him.

Squinting up at the edge of the roof, Isaac focused on the front eaves and saw that a portion of it was gone. The grenade had landed very close to the sniper. Perhaps it had been a direct hit.

Then, as Isaac watched aghast, the terrorist rose into full view a few feet to one side of the blown-apart front eaves of the roof. He was dazed. His mouth hung open.

Transfixed, Isaac saw that he was only a boy, perhaps fifteen years old. He had no weapon now, and the right side of his body ran with blood. Isaac saw that his right arm was completely gone, and the shoulder gushed rivulets of blood.

Sickened and yet relieved, Isaac rose. He heard his walkie-talkie give the kibbutz's code word for all clear, and out of the corner of his eye he saw other kibbutz workers coming out from their positions. Everyone advanced cautiously, as if the diminutive terrorist could raise his remaining arm and somehow turn them all to stone.

Behind him, he heard the *mazkir* call, "Medic!" A ladder was being carried to the building. The terrorist, now looking down on his adversaries with tears, stood his ground at the edge of the roof. He seemed to be wanting someone to finish him off or perhaps he had totally lost his grip. Isaac's heart went out to the boy.

Several people, including a medical corpsman from the kibbutz infirmary and a heavily armed army officer, were climbing onto the roof. Isaac heard the walkie-talkie bark, "Watch him, now! Watch him!" they still feared the young terrorist, and they had every right to. He might have a bomb or another weapon attached to his body. He might even have a knife and the strength to use it on the Israeli doctor.

But suddenly the boy collapsed, keeling right over at the roof's edge and nearly falling to the ground. The corpsman and soldier were now on the roof, eyeing the silent figure as they approached, ever alert to the many tricks that were part of the terrorists' murderous trade.

Convinced that the matter was over, Isaac decided to enter the nursery. He was the closest one to the door.

Carefully calling out the coded all-clear before opening the door, he made doubly sure that the walkie-talkie message had gotten through. Then he knocked and identified himself before turning the doorknob.

He looked into the eyes of an ashen-faced young woman sitting bolt upright in a straight chair. She held a submachine gun aimed right at his stomach, and she stared uncomprehendingly into his face. Her long, brown hair hung perfectly straight, framing eyes that burned like laser beams and nostrils that flared with fear. For a moment Isaac thought he was a dead man.

Elaborately casual, Isaac leaned his rifle against the doorjamb and smiled. "Well, I'm glad that's over," he said, hoping that the young lady had control of her trigger finger. "We got him with a grenade. He's not dead. A corpsman is attending to him now. You can relax."

Isaac chattered nervously, wondering if the aim of that machine gun would ever come off the center of his belt buckle, but finally he perceived the woman's body relaxing and her steady gaze softening. As she put the gun down on the floor beside her chair, Isaac at last took a deep breath.

Looking at him, she said simply, "I'm Rebecca." Then she burst into tears. She fairly leaped out of her chair then, screaming and crying, and threw herself on Isaac, who caught her in his arms. At that moment the children burst through the door into the front room and surrounded them. As he held Rebecca, Isaac noticed that the children were not nearly so depleted as the girl by the experience. All children play war games, and to them this must have been just another one. "We got him! We got him!" shouted an older boy, like the triumphant winner of a game of hide-and-seek.

In the next few minutes, people kept entering the small nursery and picking up the children to soothe them, though they didn't appear overly frightened. A few mothers came in, sobbing and clutching at their young, but the youngsters didn't seem to see the need for their emotion. Most of them had been through this sort of thing before, and in their short lifetimes no one had successfully assaulted the kibbutz. Because of the never ending defense drills and the tenacity of the workers of the land, there had never been a casualty at this particular kibbutz.

The door was closed on the scene of the terrorist being carried past the nursery on a stretcher, and everything began to return to normal. Some of the children had already lost interest in the dramatic activities and were back in the other room getting out the toys. Workers were sweeping the walkway in front of the nursery and returning it to its usual immaculate state, and a stonemason was already on the roof examining the damage to the eaves.

But in the midst of all the activity, Isaac still held Rebecca.

It felt good to him. She was soft, yielding. Her small body, her hair against his chin, her warmth, were all so different from the frantic brush with death he had just endured. He felt he could hold onto her all day. He wasn't really perceiving her as a woman at all—she was just something to be close to that wouldn't kill him.

"What is your name?" asked her light, clear voice unexpectedly in his ear.

Startled out of his reverie of security and rest, Isaac released her quickly and stepped back.

"My name is Isaac," he said woodenly, as if speaking to a customs official or some kind of interrogator. He was not at all himself. "I work in the fields," he told her.

It was a large kibbutz, and though they may have seen each other before, Isaac didn't remember her. Studying her face for the first time now, he saw that she had returned to normal repose. Her cheeks were flushed, but her eyes were relaxed. She stood looking up at him with a kind of admiration, but behind her steady look she seemed shy and inhibited.

Isaac became conscious of his sweaty field clothing and the dirt all over his face. His hands were black with a mixture of soil, sand, and sweat, and his black hair was wet and stringy with the effort he had made outside. His face took on an apologetic look, as if he were going to say, "I'm sorry for coming in

19

looking like this," and he smiled a little at the thought of it.

Rebecca returned the small, tense smile and said quietly, "Thank you for saving our lives."

Isaac nodded, as if she had thanked him for delivering the groceries. Somehow he couldn't follow all that was going on between them at this strange moment, and he assumed that the heavy atmosphere between them was due to the tension of the past hour. He looked at her blankly.

At that moment a woman Rebecca's age burst through the door and seized her, virtually crying with relief and saying, "Rebecca, Rebecca, I was so worried! Oh, Rebecca, Rebecca!" And on it went as the two of them embraced.

People were leaving the nursery after assuring themselves that there was no cause for further concern, and Isaac joined the departing crowd. He was at the doorway when he heard her speak again. She said quietly (and her voice somehow traveled right through he noisy, gathered crowd), "Isaac, wait."

He waited in the doorway as she stepped around some people to get to him. He hoped, both out of embarrassment and out of an awareness that he had done nothing heroic, that she wasn't going to make a big scene of crediting him with a rescue. The overwhelming fear that had clutched at him behind the sculpture was his clearest memory of the whole incident. He certainly didn't want to be awarded any medals. He had merely sweated out the crisis like everyone else. The man who had thrown the hand grenade, God bless his skill, would be properly certified as the hero, and Isaac just wanted to go off by himself.

When Rebecca reached him, she looked up again into his face and she seemed to understand exactly what he was thinking. She had not come to be overly gracious, he saw at once, but just to say one more thank you. He felt relieved as she simply nodded her approval of him, this time with a warm smile.

And then she did something very strange. Glancing down, she picked up his two hands in hers and held them for a moment, looking at them. Again he was conscious of how soiled they were. Then she looked at his face with an entirely different, grave expression, one that he could not fathom. Raising his hands, she placed them on her face, on her cheeks, holding them there with her own hands.

He watched her uncomprehendingly, not really feeling her face under his hands, and not understanding why she was doing this.

Then she released his hands, and he gently lifted them from her face, studying her eyes all the while. His hands found their way to his sides again, but he was unable to move. He saw the marks of the dirt on her cheeks where his hands had been.

Then suddenly she turned away and was lost

in the crowd. Isaac left the nursery in total be-wilderment.

THREE

Isaac had a bad night. Normally he slept beautifully, his small room cooled by the light breezes from the Sea of Galilee just past the trees to the north of the kibbutz. His body was usually aching for rest after his normal day of backbreaking labor in the fields, good fellowship and singing, and nourishing meals from the kibbutz commissary. Just getting into bed was a little like going to heaven. Isaac had always felt, and he never had trouble falling asleep at the kibbutz.

That had not been true in New York City, where he was brought up. Like a great many American immigrants to Israel, he slept better in the Holy Land than in exile.

Isaac had been raised in a Jewish neighborhood among Jewish people who lived out their Jewishness to a degree where it became a strange conceit. At a very tender age he had realized that his family considered themselves to be of the best of all possible races of people, but sometimes he wondered. His uncles almost boasted of their own emigration from

Europe—how they had been smart enough to leave before Hitler's rise to power, and how they had found the society and commerce of the New World hardly even a challenge,.

They were all very successful in business and the professions, and they almost swaggered in their collective accomplishments. But Isaac knew better. At least a few members of the family had not been smart enough to leave Europe in time; there were people missing. Isaac had aunts without uncles to go with them, and cousins living in the wrong households. There were no grandparents; "They died in the old country" was the incomplete explanation.

The missing relatives had died, Isaac knew, in the gas chambers of Auschwitz, Dachau, and Bergen-Belsen; they had been exterminated like vermin by the Third Reich, and Isaac had secretly wept for them.

In bed at night he would wonder about the characters of the missing people. Had his uncle Morris's wife ("We lost track of her when the family was separated at the train station") been a good woman? Had she been beautiful, creative, kind, and warm? Uncle Morris had pictures of her, which he showed to no one, and Isaac could not imagine the face of this missing aunt. Had her death been merciful? Had she been taken on the train to a quick execution, or did she have to work for the Nazis? Had she been beaten or raped? Had Uncle Morris known her destination as he stood, restrained by machine guns at some country railroad depot, watching his wife being jammed into a cattle car?

Isaac had no cousins from that marriage. He hoped and prayed that Uncle Morris and his wife had not had children at all, rather than imagining what might have happened to them. Morris was closemouthed, and no one asked him about his family. That subject was taboo; there was no point in pursuing it. Isaac did not even know the name of his deceased aunt, and Uncle Morris, who had never remarried but continued to live with those old photographs, never revealed it.

Isaac's parents had immigrated to America long before Hitler came to power, and they were the most Americanized of all the family, as far as young Isaac could see. They spoke Yiddish at home, and English with a rich accent elsewhere, but they were in tune with their times. Isaac's father was successful in business—he manufactured clothing—and his mother had never worked outside their home. His older brother and sister had made a success of American life, his brother as a lawyer, and his sister as a housewife and mother. Isaac was the strange one in the family, a highly sensitive, emotional child given to a great deal of quiet and solitude. ("What can you expect of the last child?" he heard Uncle Morris ask his mother in whispered Yiddish one night. And he had hoped Morris had not gained his wisdom about children from personal experience as a father.)

At such times as his Bar Mitzvah, Isaac would be most disturbed about his family and its missing parts. When all his relatives gathered, the "holes" in the group were very apparent. Though the rabbi had put his arm around Isaac in the synagogue and declared to the joyful multitude, *"Am Yisroel chai!"*—"The Jewish people live!"—Isaac felt hollow inside.

There was a Jewish way to grow up in Isaac's community, and he followed it to the letter, all the while wondering if there were not other plausible ways to grow up. He joined the AZA, a boys' club of Jewish teenagers vaguely dedicated to Israel and the Jewish ideals; and he played a lot of basketball with curly headed, dark-skinned Jewish athletes who whipped any other ethnic group hands down, despite their lack of height. Once in a while he joined in street fights against the Italians, who lived a few blocks over, or the Blacks, who failed to appreciate, Isaac always thought, that the Jews were more than just white. But Isaac did not like the fighting (and neither did the Italians or the Blacks, as far as he could tell), and he usually stayed clear of it.

He ate Jewish food and kept to the rather uncertain kosher laws his family kept. ("A little bacon once in a great while—God will forgive you," his father had assured him.) And he never dates a *shiksa*, a Gentile girl.

Actually, Isaac stayed pretty much away from all girls, not being able to understand them, and kept his mind on schoolwork and sports. His father urged him to study hard and "become something in this world," but as a youngster Isaac well knew that what his father wanted him to become was a partner in his business. His older brother had shied away from that, and Isaac also had little interest in it. Why would a man devote his life to making clothes for people? There must be something more to living than that. Isaac's father hated that reasoning and simply assured his last son and last hope, "You'll know better someday; someday you'll know better." And he would solemnly conclude on some occasions, "You'll appreciate me when I'm gone."

When Isaac graduated from high school he looked like "a nice Jewish boy." Of ordinary height and build, with dark curly hair and deep-set brown eyes, he was the type of young Jew who faded into any Jewish crowd but would stand out embarrassingly at a Gentile country club. He had that slightly foreign look that Jews possess in every country, including modern Israel.

The real agony in Isaac's family came over his not wanting to go to college. "Are you going to *schlep* boxes for some Irish trucker, huh?" his father shouted acidly. "Are you going to live off the fat of the land, *chacham?*" His father's sarcasm was endless on the point, making Isaac realize that he was truly only an appendage of his father's existence, responsible to make his father look as good as possible to the rest of the world.

At the more terrible moments, his mother would intercede, "Let him alone. He's all right, let him alone."

Isaac's mother had a quiet wisdom and a long-suffering patience with her overbearing husband. Isaac had her inner spirit of peace and complacency, and they more or less understood each other. But when she did inquire of him one day during the summer following his graduation, "So what will it be for you?" Isaac didn't know.

"I have no plans," he told her, as kindly as he could.

Isaac went to Israel in the fall after graduation. It had been suggested to him by Zvi Cohen, a "reverse immigrant" (he had emigrated from Israel to the United States). Zvi worked as a Hebrew teacher, athletic coach, and all-around inspiration to the Jewish youth at the community center where Isaac played basketball and did his fighting. Zvi had confided to Isaac that life was difficult in Israel and that he himself had found that he was simply not a pioneer. He had been born in Israel long before the 1948 independence and had grown up fighting the Arabs and the British and the sundry Turks, Syrians, Jordanians, Lebanese, and others whose inevitable presence always kept life on the keen edge of terror in the Holy Land.

Zvi had become exhausted with it all, married an American girl who covered Israel as a correspondent for an American news bureau, and took what his fellow Israelis regarded as the easy way out. But Zvi worked tirelessly for Israel in the United States, mainly recruiting young Jews to go there and build the land. He felt he did Israel a greater service in recommending the country to Americans than in continuing to defend it personally, and Isaac thought he was right. Someday he would return to the promised land, Zvi told Isaac. "I promised God I would die over there," he explained, "and it's becoming an easier thing to do these days. I'll go back after I catch my breath."

Zvi was practical. He told Isaac, "Look, it's a hard life. The Jews in Israel are mixed company, from everywhere and anywhere. They work too hard, get too little for it, and are always nervous. The whole world hates them, and you can depend on it, but that has always been our honor, hasn't it? The Arabs are a barbaric people who think only in terms of their own possessions and their own power. They have no learning, no comprehension, no God, and they're always on every side of you over there. I had Arab friends, of course, but by and large it's like living on the stretch of land between two armies. I can recommend it."

You're the worst salesman I've ever heard," Isaac told him, even as he thought seriously about signing up to go to Israel.

"I'm telling you the truth. You have the Gentiles to lie to you," Zvi told him with a knowing smile. "Go there. You won't regret it."

Isaac's father was caught in a trap by all this. He could hardly object strenuously to his son's undertaking so Jewish an endeavor as traveling to the Holy Land to give some of his life to its reconstruction. On the other hand, what kind of business was that for a Jew?

"You are not an Oriental!" he burst out at Isaac one night. "You are an American. Stay here! Your family needs you." Isaac couldn't accept it. He had never felt that his family, or America, needed him in any particular way. On the other hand, Zvi had assured him that Israel needed him—and every other Jew that was available—very badly. And as he had no better plans, he decided to go.

Zvi had arranged for Isaac to become an archaeological worker, digging in the immensely interesting ruins of Israel, where pieces of almost any Western civilization of any age might turn up. Isaac started in Galilee, where Roman artifacts lay practically on the surface, and eventually graduated to the Temple site, after the 1967 War. The real history of the Jewish people could be found beside the Western Wall of the Temple, called the "Wailing Wall."

And it was there, after digging in the soil of Israel, that Isaac first experienced deep, untroubled sleep. He slept wonderfully, waking up at about four o'clock to beat the Jerusalem sun. He would watch the Jerusalem stone turn golden twelve hours later as that remarkable sun set. He learned what it was to work hard, to feel the sweat run down his body, and to know the kind of rest and victory that comes to those who earn them every night.

He attended the *Ulpan*, the almost cruel school of the Hebrew language, where a man could nearly die in the cafeteria line if he forgot the word for *meat*. He was ostracized at first, to the point of wanting to say to the harried, over scurrying Israelis around him, "Hey, I've come to help you make a country!" But when he passed their test of endurance—when they saw that he was not going to crawl back to air-conditioned America after all—he became one of them. It gave him a true feeling of having a family, something which he now knew he had somehow always lacked. Hitler had dealt a more majestic blow to the Jewish people than even his incomprehensible thinning of their numbers; he had affected their collective psychology so that their very ability to commune, to love, was perverted. People cannot remain normal during the constant work of forgetting. Whether or not they survived the holocaust, they all eventually died from it.

Isaac matured into an Israeli, strong of body, with a tense but dependable temperament. With the haughty and grand aloofness of a true *Sabra*, a native son of the promised land, he snubbed American Jewish tourists and, to him, their ridiculous Christian counterparts. He spat out Hebrew at them as though he knew no English, but in more sincere moments he was glad for their interest and commitment to the land of the Jews. Even the Christians, with their gospel picture of Israel, proved to be genuinely interested in the Holy Land and its special aura of promise and excitement. The Christian ministers, spouting their incredible versions of prophecy and waiting around for the coming of their King, seemed impressed with what the relative handful of immigrants had done with this land in a generation. Many of them, Isaac knew, contributed cold cash— the ultimate American commitment and the hardest of all to part with—for the rebuilding of Israel. Isaac was moved by that, though he inwardly pitied what he considered their esoteric philosophies about the land and the Kingdom to come.

If they thought Jesus Christ was coming back, well and good, Isaac figured. Israel needed men, after all, and He would be welcome. Hopefully He would be more tactful this time.

Isaac's ideas about Jesus were formed through his slight acquaintance with what the Prophet had said—mainly the Sermon on the Mount and other widely quoted snippets of the New Testament—and his own observation of American Christianity. The former, Isaac could not help but appreciate for its own sake. Jesus was a brilliant Man, superior to many a philosopher Isaac was acquainted with. But He had chosen a hopeless cause when He had decided to sanctify Gentiles.

A Christian missionary had tried to "witness" to Isaac at one point in Israel, but Isaac laughed it off. The missionary declared that Jesus had come to the Jews to make Christians of them, and Isaac replied in Yiddish, *"Das velt mir noch"*—"That we really need!" He had agreed with the missionary that Jesus was a good soul, but he could not buy the idea that the modern Jews were to follow His gospel. "We have seen for thousand years how bad it is," Isaac argued.

Isaac wrote home now and then, and even managed a visit to America during his long years in the Holy Land. But he found New York City, his family, and America in general extremely cold and shallow compared to his new homeland. "I don't understand what you're doing with your lives," he told his family. "You're just wasting time. This country—this shopping center between oceans—will survive without you. Come home with me and plant some trees!"

They didn't like his attitude, nor his beard, nor his fluent Hebrew. Isaac had somehow become too Jewish for them, and they hardly knew him. At the community center there was a new generation of basketball players, but they didn't play basketball in the evening anymore. They smoked marijuana and went off with the girls and all dressed like hoboes. Israel felt that he had left American just in time, that he had jumped off a sinking ship.

Zvi was still there, and Isaac conveyed his heartfelt thanks. He and Zvi strolled the hall of the community center, speaking Hebrew and looking askance at the goings-on. Isaac asked Zvi if he were ready to come back to the promised land now, but he recognized in the sad eyes of the worn-out Israeli the signs of middle-age lethargy. Zvi would not be coming home after all, Isaac understood, despite his promise to God. The Americans had gotten him as firmly as the Israelis had gotten Isaac. Zvi was the last one to whom he said good-bye as he boarded the El Al 747 for his trip back home to Israel, and he knew he would never forget that look of envy in Zvi's tired eyes.

During that visit home Isaac had missed the Yom Kippur War. He had followed the action confidently in the newspapers and on

TV, sure that the Israelis would rout the enemy as in 1967, but things went harder for them this time. As the three weeks of the war went on, the Israelis came out on top, as Isaac had known they would, but obviously this had been a much harder fight. He saw with satisfaction the surrounding of the Egyptian Third Army in the Sinai by General Sharon, and the predicted days in advance for his father that the Russians would get the war stopped before Israel could progress to occupy Cairo. "Visit Israel and see the pyramids," he chortled to his family.

Isaac had enough acquaintance with Israeli servicemen to know how things were on the battlefields, and he wasn't worried. The Egyptian was no solider, he knew, and had nothing really to fight about. The Syrians were tough, bullyish personalities with no skill and little grasp on modern warfare. With Russian weaponry and advice, the enemy could be tediously lengthy about losing the war, but they must lose. "And," as Isaac told his father in all sincerity, "if they fight us every year for a thousand years, they will lose every war."

Isaac had now become the swaggering one in his family, he realized, and he was glad to leave them and go home again. El Al was guaranteeing safe passage even while the final days of the conflict wound down, and Russia had predictably come around to rescue what was left of their war materiel. Isaac felt personally proud of Israel and glad to be part of the country.

But he was not at all prepared for the grief and depression in Jerusalem when he got back. People were weeping in the streets! Isaac, like the foreigner he really was, had not stopped to calculate the losses of Israel—twenty-five hundred young men who represented almost every family in the land. Everyone seemed to have lost someone he knew, and there was an attitude of hopelessness among the confident people he had left only weeks before. Military funerals filled the days with sorrow in Jerusalem and throughout the land. Jeremiah's Lamentations were being relived, and Isaac was stricken.

A new mood of quiet desperation was abroad in the land, Isaac could see after his return. "How long can we continue to hold them off?" everyone seemed to be asking. "Why should we have to live this way?" The industrious, self-assured pioneers he had left only weeks earlier had changed into dazed, bewildered doubters. It was a tangible thing, an atmosphere that pervaded every crowd on every street corner. "How can we continue?"

A great deal of spiritual talk was going on; God would prevail, and through His power His chosen people would always survive. Many families turned back to the Talmud and other religious books, and the rabbis spoke of biblical prophecies guaranteeing the security of the promised land. But it was also very apparent that Israel could not even afford to *win* such wars; the cost of fighting at all was far too high for the small society of land builders. If such fighting continued, Israel would eventually be worn down to a last few who would resemble the first-century suicides at Masada.

In his own mind, Isaac took on a new mission. New territory, reaching into Syria from the Golan Heights northeast of the Sea of Galilee, had been occupied. Israelis were needed to people that buffer zone, just to be there when the Syrians came again, as they always had and always would. Settlers were already moving northward, and Isaac applied to join them.

There were so many volunteers, however, that Isaac had to settle for the kibbutz located just to the south of the sea, where he now resided. It was as close as he could come to the future action, but at least it provided an opportunity to protect the land. The Kibbutz had seen some terrorist action, Isaac had warned, and it was quite close to the borders of both Jordan and Syria. Isaac rejoiced in his assignment.

Life settled back to normalcy, that is, normalcy for Israel—bombings by terrorists; unexpected searches in public near border checkpoints; steady, unrelenting security procedures everywhere in the land. A girl could not walk into a movie theater without enduring a look into her pocketbook by a soldier; hitch-hiking along the roads would occasion the attention of local police or army personnel. No one could pass into the Old City of Jerusalem to approach the Western Wall without passing a checkpoint. Everyone, it seemed, conducted steady observation of everyone else.

Isaac was now a farmer instead of an archaeologist, but it mattered little to him just how he worked or what he did. The point was to be in Israel, to uphold the land and the promises of God, to support the Jewish people. How Jews could live elsewhere, he didn't understand, except possibly in the case of Zvi, or the living-dead Uncle Morris. But to Isaac, life meant Israel. He possessed the rarest gift of the modern world—*Ohaveh Yisroel*, the love of Israel—and his heart was full of purpose.

Isaac came to know some Arab citizens of Israel in his new locale. He visited wholly Arab cities, including Nazareth, reputedly the town where Jesus was raised. He certainly saw a difference between the Arabs of Israel and the demons who came over the borders. Live and let live seemed to be the philosophy of the Arabs of the land, and he had more than once heard an Arab state that the Jews were doing a fine job with Israel.

But then came the attempts of Jerusalem Jews to pray on the Temple Mount near the Muslim Dome of the Rock. Riots in West Bank towns erupted, and the Arabs within the land became something of a threat to Israel. Isaac resolved to take his Arabs as he found them—one by one—and to make no judgments. They were people, too, with hopes and dreams, and children and land. Some were religious, in the Muslim way, and Isaac could not, in truth, draw a logical difference between religions. He loved Judaism; but then, he was a Jew. He knew little of the Hebrew Scriptures and nothing of the Koran, and he tended to respect the Muslims and their faith. The secular Arab he simply could not understand, but the Arab who at least believed in a higher power he could abide.

And so Isaac became a modern Israeli, a man with a vision about his land, a watchful eye for his enemies, and a strong back for his work. He earned little and spent little; he contemplated God in a vague but sincere way, and he always lived fully, ready to die with a sense of accomplishment at any moment.

But this morning Isaac was tired and discouraged because of a long night of terrible dreams. He had never been one to worry about emotional troubles; his mind had always been dependably efficient, and his feelings moderate on most things. He never experienced deep depression, and he had become used to a clear conscience and good nights of deep sleep in Israel.

But last night he had heard explosions in

his room and seen one-armed children racing about in terror and confusion. Time after time, he had awakened, afraid to close his eyes again, seeing always that astonished face on the roof, the accusing eyes. There was a vision of a woman, her face streaked with dirt, and the sound of more explosions until Isaac thought he would cry out and wake the others.

Somewhere in the middle of his nightmares it was suddenly morning and he lay awake aching.

He had slept too long—it was already dawn. But he knew he could not work this morning. He felt as thought he had been through a beating.

With a firm resolve, Isaac got up, dressed, and went immediately to the kibbutz infirmary. He at least had to know if the youngster with one arm was still alive.

FOUR

The infirmary was a one-story wooden building where Isaac had been treated many times for aches and pains and sniffles. The kibbutz physician, Dr. David ben Judah, was a crabby European refugee who, like Isaac himself, had found his life in Israel. He had adopted his almost romantic name in his new homeland, and no one knew much about who he really was or what his European background and education entailed.

One thing was certain—Dr. ben Judah was one in a million as a doctor.

The doctor could perform any sort of surgery, it seemed, and he preferred to treat all kibbutz casualties—military and civilian—right at the infirmary, rather than send them to Tiberias or Haifa, as some northern kibbutzim did. David ben Judah trusted no other doctor, Israeli or immigrant, and he was genuinely and justifiably revered throughout the kibbutz. His medical skills were as dependable as his bedside manner was lacking, and the crusty, old misanthrope was deeply loved.

Isaac was almost afraid to confront him that morning with an inquiry about the terrorist. Dr.

ben Judah treated patients of all sorts, and terrorists had been ministered to at this kibbutz before, but this was not to say he preferred them as patients. Isaac approached with trepidation, hoping only to find out if the young terrorist was alive.

"He's alive, Isaac," Dr. ben Judah spat out as he busied himself with some medical records on his desk. "But he won't last a day, I suppose."

Isaac sat respectfully in the doctor's cramped little office, embarrassed to be asking about the terrorist's condition, but sensing that even the grouchy ben Judah regretted the mortal injury to so young an invader. The doctor said nothing for a time, but then he looked up at Isaac with eyes that reflected humanity and compassion.

"How do they get that way so young?" he asked in heavily accented Hebrew. "He told us his story. He does nothing but practice with a rifle; he lives to kill Israelis. He was raised by terrorists and groomed as a terrorist. He thinks we're devils, savages."

The doctor looked back at his work with a sigh as Isaac waited for some understanding of the terrorist's condition. Looking up, the doctor understood Isaac's unspoken request. "He has a severe spinal cord cut, up by the back of his neck. His right shoulder is full of shrapnel. His arm is gone, and he's lost a lot of blood. He has internal injuries everywhere; massive bleeding; there's just no place to begin. I'm sorry," he added.

"I'm sorry, too," Isaac repeated, feeling somehow as though he were losing a brother. He hoped he had not overdone his concern in front of the passionately antiterrorist doctor. Isaac just could not forget that youthful face, that utter bewilderment, the blood, and the missing arm. The grotesque memory just would not fade away.

Doctor ben Judah seemed to understand what he was thinking. "He's sedated now. He can talk. He regains consciousness now and then. But he can't be moved, not even touched. He's paralyzed—what's left of him. We've given him blood and antibiotics. There's a very small chance that the cord will heal, but I doubt it. More likely he'll die very soon." The doctor paused, with an unseeing look back at his papers. "I hope he dies, Isaac, because there won't be much for him if he lives. I'm sorry."

Isaac waited before asking the doctor if he might see the young man, not knowing if it was either proper or possible. The doctor again sensed the unspoken request. "You're not his first visitor this morning," he said. "You can go in if you like." He turned back to his papers, indicating that the interview, like the patient, was finished business.

Isaac made his way down the hallway of the infirmary, knowing where he would find the patient. There was only one real hospital room in the little infirmary, since the doctor treated outpatients almost exclusively. When the flu hit the kibbutz, or when injured soldiers were brought from the nearby border, a recreation building was pressed into service.

There was silence, as complete as death itself, as Isaac opened the door of the terrorist's room. Somehow Isaac thought he would confront bloody sheets and the horrible stump of the armless shoulder when he looked at the terrorist. But in the darkened room he saw only a normal-looking patient asleep under sheets, his face composed as he rested.

To his surprise, Isaac also saw Rebecca sitting quietly in a straight chair in the corner of the room away from the bed.

Rebecca looked at him with eyes that Isaac immediately recognized from his dreams. He was almost surprised that her face was clean again and not marked with the dirt from his hands, as it had been in his visions during the night.

Rebecca said quietly, "I knew you would come."

Feeling very strange, Isaac could only think to say, "How is he?"

Rebecca glanced at the bed, as if to be sure that the patient was still asleep and not overhearing the conversation. "Did you talk to the doctor?" she asked. Isaac nodded gravely, and Rebecca knew that his rhetorical question was answered. They were together in a death watch.

As Rebecca sat unmoving, Isaac drew nearer to the bed, drawn by a force that made him want to see the face of the terrorist. He assured himself that the boy was breathing, although slowly, and as he approached he saw a peaceful, dark-skinned countenance, the same as the face of any Arab boy anywhere in Israel. There was no distortion from pain, and Isaac was grateful.

Suddenly, as if from nowhere, tears filled Isaac's eyes, and he turned from the boy, his face wet. Rebecca watched him as he dried his cheeks with his sleeve and suppressed a sob that threatened to burst from his chest.

He shook his head back and forth, as if to clear it of such disabling emotions, and then he suddenly felt Rebecca's embrace. Some instinctual part of his mind dutifully reminded him of this woman and her embrace, how it had felt the same yesterday morning when he had confronted her in the nursery. She had come quietly across the room when she had seen Isaac about to lose control of himself, taking him in her arms as a mother would.

They both just held onto each other, regaining their feelings.

"Get me a priest," a quiet voice whispered behind them.

They both jumped, realizing the terrorist had spoken.

"Get me a priest," he said again, with furrowed forehead. He seemed to have little difficulty talking, but nothing moved but his jaw. His eyes were closed, his face still pointed straight up toward the ceiling.

Isaac jumped to the bedside, realizing the boy had addressed him in Hebrew. He asked incongruously, "How do you feel? Are you all right?"

The boy whispered, "Jesus can heal me. Get me a priest."

Incredulous, Isaac looked at Rebecca.

"Go and get him a priest," she said firmly.

Isaac found himself back out in the hallway, heading for the office of Dr. ben Judah and his telephone. He had no idea whom he was going to call, or how he would come up with a priest, of all things. He wondered fleetingly if the boy were merely talking as if in a dream, maybe seeing some vision of a healing Jesus. Perhaps Isaac was wasting his time, but Rebecca had seemed to take the request seriously.

Isaac tapped on the doctor's door and waited quite a while until he heard a grump "Yes?"

He entered and simply blurted out the boy wanted a priest. Did the doctor know where they might find one? Isaac told the doctor the boy believed Jesus could heal him.

"Well, maybe He can," muttered Dr. ben Judah. "I certainly can't."

"But where in the world can we find a priest fast enough?"

"I can give you a number to call in Tiberias. It's a Christian mission. They'll probably send somebody out here. Tell them to send a Jewish Christian so that they don't question him at the gate. We've had enough Gentiles around here to last us a while."

"But he wants a *priest*, not a missionary!" Isaac objected, betraying his disgust at the idea of a Jewish Christian on the kibbutz.

"I don't know where to find a priest, Isaac, and what's the difference? Can you understand that the boy will be dead by sundown? Get him somebody that will make a prayer for him, and he'll die a little happier. Excuse me now, I'm busy." With that he jotted down the phone number, gestured to the hallway phone, and turned back to his work.

Isaac had a pretty good idea of whom he was calling on the phone. He had heard of the Christian group in Tiberias that studied the New Testament and included a few misguided Jews among their number. How Jews could become Christians, Isaac never understood, despite hearing the arguments of the missionaries on several occasions. He bore the Jewish Christians no personal malice, but he definitely preferred not to associate with them. In this case, however, he was willing to extend himself, although it occurred to him that they could just send in somebody from the kibbutz to pretend he was a priest. For the sake of the terrorist, they could fake it, couldn't they? How would he know the difference if they brought in a Jew, anyway? But Isaac immediately rejected that thinking, purely on the emotional basis that the youngster deserved his last request. They would come up with a believer in Jesus, even if he didn't have priestly robes.

On the phone he was a bit nervous. This wasn't his cup of tea. To the man who answered the phone, he explained the situation at the kibbutz and the terrorist's request. Then he asked for a Jewish Christian, saying plainly that they were concerned only with the terrorist and that the kibbutz would tolerate no evangelism. "He thinks Jesus can heal him," he concluded.

"He's right about that," said the accommodating voice from the mission.

"Well, fine," Isaac said, trying not to sound sarcastic. "He really asked for a priest, rather than just a missionary."

"All Christians are priests," the voice said confidently.

Isaac felt some odd affinity for this man with his self-assured tone and his obvious spiritual understanding. The Hebrew was native, it seemed to Isaac, though he had trouble picking out the infinite numbers of shaded dialects of the Holy Land. And the man spoke to Isaac as though he had called for some routine purpose, rather than with this outlandish request. Isaac also noticed no trace of animosity at the idea of talking with a terrorist.

"Are you Jewish?" Isaac asked. When he received an affirmative answer, he asked, "Can you come yourself?"

There was a pause as Isaac realized he had unintentionally committed himself in some way to this person on the other end of the telephone connection. He had betrayed that he was impressed by the missionary's manner and in some way he was. He knew that Christians had a tough life in Israel; they were shunned, sometimes even derided publicly. He couldn't help recognizing that nevertheless the voice was warm and accepting.

"I'll be honored to come," the missionary said. "I'll come as soon as I can get a ride. Can you meet me at the kibbutz gate in an hour?"

Isaac agreed to the arrangements and was sorry as soon as he'd hung up the phone. Why should he have to walk through the kibbutz with this person? What if somebody knew the missionary? The last thing Isaac wanted was to be seen with a Jewish Christian, no matter what the circumstances. He would have preferred to have met a Muslim at the gate.

Isaac went back to the terrorist's room to tell Rebecca what had transpired. He had another surprise as he entered—Rebecca was holding the left hand of the youngster and they were talking. Isaac tiptoed to a corner of the room, unseen by the boy but noticed by Rebecca, who smiled at him.

In a slow voice, the terrorist was telling her about his family and his past. What Isaac could hear of it was commonplace. Certainly Rebecca was not trying to get information from the terrorist; the army would look over the bodies of other terrorists and, as always, place the raid at its accurate source. They probably would not retaliate for this gang warfare intrusion; such incidents were commonplace near the border. The only thing surprising was that the terrorists had somehow reached the kibbutz without being detected. That lapse would be studied and the leak plugged, and life would go on as usual.

Then Isaac realized that Rebecca was merely offering comfort to the boy. Her concern for others and her depth of caring were obvious, written all over her face as the boy talked; she had a great deal of love, and it seemed to exude from her in every direction.

As Isaac watched her holding the boy's hand, he recognized another feeling within himself that he had known was inevitable from the first moment that he saw her. He felt her presence as a woman, and he himself wanted to hold that tender hand. He knew very well that he was falling in love with her.

In truth, he wasn't all that impressed with the feeling. It had come and gone fleetingly before in his life, toward girls who had not even noticed his presence. Rebecca had a wonderful sensitivity about her, but Isaac thought that she probably had not even noticed him as a man. For a woman to embrace a man in a situation such as he and Rebecca had found themselves in yesterday was a natural part of womanliness. He had little hope of her developing any real feeling for him. But he thought he might pass the nursery again some morning and see if she would like to talk with him.

"Isaac, he wants to talk to you," Rebecca said suddenly; she was standing right in front of him. Isaac jumped; for he was so lost in his thoughts that he had not seen her cross the room. Noticing a light in her eyes, he hoped she had not read his thoughts with that uncanny way of hers. As he stood up and went to the bedside, she gave him the slightest hint of a smile. His mind was full of her face and her graceful manner, but he could not find any words to speak to her.

He leaned a little toward the boy's face so that the boy could see him more easily. With some difficulty the boy turned his head slightly and faced Isaac. "Did you throw the grenade?" he asked simply.

About an hour later, Isaac had returned with the missionary. Rebecca still maintained her vigil in the terrorist's room, and the four of them convened together. They made an odd group: Isaac, the American Jew; Rebecca, emigrated from some European land; Joshua, the Israeli Jewish Christian, probably spreading as much discomfort as he himself felt; and the Palestinian terrorist, near death but conscious in his bed.

It had been a difficult hour for Isaac. First he had assured the youngster that he had not thrown the grenade that blew off the boy's arm and put him in such misery. "I was behind the sculpture on the pavement," Isaac had explained calmly. "I did not throw the grenade or shoot at you at all. You could just as easily have shot at me." The terrorist seemed satisfied, barely able to nod his head, but more willing to converse with Isaac.

As they talked further, Isaac learned that the boy was not a Christian believer of any sort—he just thought that somehow Jesus could heal him. He vaguely knew the events of Jesus' life in Israel, and he remembered that healing was a part of that ministry. He also was well aware that he was dying.

Isaac was relieved that the boy was not a Catholic and that his requirement of a priest was not based on any special religious preference. *Priest* to this Palestinian, simply meant a representative of Jesus, and the missionary whom Isaac had called would be able to fill the bill. Maybe the missionary was right—all Christians were priests, at least when it came to a situation like this.

What the missionary was going to do when he got to the terrorist was a mystery to Isaac. He assumed the man would be sensitive enough to comfort the dying patient; he hoped there wouldn't be any last rites ceremony in the hospital room. He also hoped there wouldn't be any kind of evangelizing, for it would seem too much like taking advantage of the boy, Isaac doubted if the patient was thinking clearly at all, and he hoped the interview would be comforting.

Then Isaac had gone to the kibbutz gate and had his second difficult interview of the hour. There was no problem with the sentry or the people they passed as they walked to the infirmary; Isaac was glad he had asked for a Jewish Christian, because Joshua looked like any Israeli visitor to the area. Certainly no one looked strangely at Isaac, as they would have if he were accompanied by a Gentile. Isaac felt a wave of relief that the man at the gate wasn't wearing clerical robes, but he immediately realized that the idea was silly. He knew very well that the missionaries of Tiberias were not demonstrative, and he could certainly understand that. And the Evangelicals of Israel didn't wear robes or perform rituals. That was half the problem with them; they looked so normal that they couldn't be picked out until they actually started brandishing their Bibles and talking about Christ.

The difficulty came in his talk with Joshua as they walked along. Isaac had begun, "I don't think it would be in good taste for you to talk a lot about Christianity to this boy."

Joshua had replied, "I thought you would feel that way, but that's what I have to do." They walked on in silence for a while, measuring each other.

Joshua, tall and spare with a full beard, was dark and obviously Israeli, and Isaac thought for a fleeting moment that this must have been what Jesus looked like. The face of the missionary was open and his eyes kind. Despite their philosophical differences, Isaac couldn't help but see the man's wisdom, and of course he appreciated his willingness to come to the kibbutz at a moment's notice. All the same, he didn't want the missionary to start telling him about Jesus, and he avoided further mention of religion in their conversation.

The missionary dressed plainly, like the kibbutz members and Israelis in general, in a white open shirt and faded cotton trousers. His clothes were clean but shabby. He smiled a lot, with his own private thoughts. Isaac could not help but like him.

When they arrived at the room, the terrorist seemed to be asleep and Rebecca was close beside the bed. Isaac introduced Joshua and Rebecca briefly and then sank into a chair. Exhausted from all the emotional goings-on, he needed a rest. He had his special troubles handling all three of them—the terrorist, before whom he somehow felt guilty; Joshua, whose oddly affecting personality was such a mismatch with his unacceptable religion; and finally, Rebecca, whom he was so strangely glad to see again. He felt like asking Dr. ben Judah for a sedative, or better, waking up to find the whole business just another disturbing dream. He almost dozed off as he sat listening to the missionary and the terrorist.

Joshua had approached the bed immediately and looked carefully at the boy. The patient's eyes opened as if on cue and he looked back curiously at his new visitor.

The boy spoke first. "Are you a priest?" he asked in a small voice.

"Yes, I am," Joshua said firmly.

"Can Jesus heal me?" the boy asked.

"Of course He can," said the missionary.

FIVE

Isaac didn't like the missionary's approach. He didn't really think Jesus could heal this boy. Like Dr. ben Judah, he thought that the boy would die very soon and he saw no reason for holding out false hopes to him.

But it was none of his affair, he knew. The boy had asked for Christian counsel, and he was getting it, for what it was worth. Perhaps the missionary felt that if the boy thought he would be healed it might help him pull through, but Isaac was extremely doubtful. He kept quiet, though, and followed the conversation. Rebecca, too, he saw, was carefully listening.

"Where did you hear about Jesus?" the missionary asked, rather professionally Isaac thought.

"An evangelist," the boy said with difficulty. "In our camp."

"In a Palestinian camp? Really?"

"He was a Palestinian. But he told us Jesus was an Israeli."

"That's true," the missionary said softly. "But He heals all men."

"He was shot," the boy continued. "One of our officers shot him. But I believed him. I loved him."

"Is he dead now?" Joshua asked.

There was a long pause as the boy's eyes closed. He seemed to drift away, and Isaac sat up suddenly, thinking the boy had died. But then his soft voice came again, "He is not dead. Jesus healed him."

"How do you know that?" the missionary asked.

"He told me. he told me that Jesus would always take care of him. His wound was healed. I saw it."

Isaac doubted the story, but he knew such tales were rampant in the Christian religion. Now he thought he understood the boy's concern about Jesus, and his belief that Jesus could heal him. It was purely his fear; he had no other choice. Why not try Jesus if you know you're going to die?

Joshua was telling the boy, "You must love the Lord, not just ask Him to heal you."

There was silence. Isaac remained quiet with some difficultly.

The boy finally said, in a very weak voice, "I don't know Him. I don't know Jesus."

"Do you want to know Him? Shall I tell you about Him?"

"Yes," said the terrorist, eyes shut tightly. "Tell me about Him."

Isaac saw that Joshua's face was tight and his eyes blazing. He was concentrating hard, and Isaac could not help realizing that, whatever their differences, he was watching a man desperately working against time. How could he possibly explain Jesus to this boy effectively, when the boy might slip away in the middle of it? What was the point? Isaac saw that the missionary closed his eyes and drew in a long, deep breath. He was praying, Isaac supposed, and that was understandable. At length, his prayers over, the missionary began to tell the terrorist about Jesus.

"He loves you," Joshua began.

"He was filled with love for everyone, and He took time to tell everyone He saw about the Kingdom of God. He healed people, and He taught them about His Father.

"He walked all over Israel, and He talked to the Jews, the Samaritans, and even the Canaanites. He talked to your people and my people—everyone in the land. He said He came to the lost sheep of the house of Israel, but He turned no one away. He healed little children, and He warned the people at the Temple that they were forgetting God.

"They killed Him finally. You must know that. But He was like your friend in the camp—God healed Him. In fact, God brought Him back to life, and He went home to His Father in heaven. He had such faith that He was not afraid to die, and He *chose* to die. He died for everyone else, so that we all could go to the Kingdom. He died for you.

"To everyone that received Him, He gave the power to be a child of God."

Joshua stopped at that point, looking intently at his silent, unmoving listener. Isaac saw that Rebecca's eyes were wet.

The boy said slowly, "I want to be a child of God."

"Tell that to God," Joshua said.

The boy made no effort to speak for a few moments. Isaac wondered if he were too weak or if he were just composing his statement to God. Rebecca leaned forward and looked at the boy. He began to speak in a whisper, "Dear God, I want to be Your child."

And then suddenly his eyes opened wide and his voice was stronger. He actually smiled as he exclaimed in a surprisingly loud voice, *"I want to be Your child!"*

The boy looked at Isaac and then at Rebecca with a triumphant look. Joshua was lost in fervent prayer, his head bowed and his eyes closed tightly. His forehead glistened with sweat.

"Jesus," the boy continued more quietly. "I love you. I believe in You. Take me to the Kingdom of God."

There was a long silence which made Isaac terribly uncomfortable. Something had happened, he knew. Perhaps the boy was just suddenly hysterical, perhaps the missionary was good at picking out the emotional part of his clients, but there was no doubt—something had happened. When he looked at Rebecca, he saw that she realized the same thing. She was staring in wonder at the boy and Joshua.

Joshua voiced his prayer aloud at this point. "Dear Father in heaven, thank You," he began. "Thank You for reaching out and touching our brother. Thank You for healing his body and saving his soul. Thank You for saving his place in the Kingdom to come. Father, You said You wanted the children to come unto You; Father, thank You for this opportunity with this child. In Jesus' name, I thank You!"

With incredulity Isaac saw that the patient was smiling and animated. He had not moved, to be sure. His body was not healed at all. But his manner, his attitude, was entirely changed. He spoke at once to the missionary in a calm, clear voice. "Will God heal my body? Will He do that for me?"

Isaac knew that was a hard question, but the missionary seemed ready for it. "He'll heal you today if that is His will for you. And if you die here in this bed, He'll still heal you today. He'll give you an entirely new body—a new arm and all the rest, better than your old body."

"I'm not afraid to die," the terrorist said.

"Today you'll be in paradise if you do," the missionary said.

At that the patient fell into a deep sleep, the smile still radiating from his glowing face.

A few minutes later Isaac and Joshua were walking back to the kibbutz gate, the "priest's" mission completed. After the boy had fallen asleep, Dr. ben Judah had looked in on his patient, jerked his head at the two men, and they had left, obeying the medical command. Rebecca had been permitted to stay in the room, but the doctor told her to be quiet and let the boy sleep. Isaac wasn't aware if Dr. ben Judah had overheard the proceedings in the room through the thin wall that separated his office from the infirmary section of the little building. In any case, he had arrived right at the conclusion of the remarkable prayer ceremonies.

Isaac felt self-conscious walking with the missionary again. Many more people were on the streets and pathways of the kibbutz living area now that the afternoon rest period was under way, and Isaac somehow thought Joshua's religion showed. But at that point he knew he would have defended Joshua in gratitude for the missionary's selfless efforts. As they walked along in silence, he hoped that Joshua was not going to start in with something like, "Now, how about you? You're going to die someday. Don't you want to go to the Kingdom of God, too?" But Joshua, seeming to sense that Isaac would not welcome his witness, said nothing.

Finally, Isaac himself broke the tension. "Is it that simple?" he asked. "Is that boy 'saved' now?" Isaac put a certain distasteful emphasis on the evangelical term "saved," as though the boy had contracted a repulsive disease.

"It's that simple, as I understand God and the Messiah," Joshua replied with his usual confident firmness.

"All he did was catch your own enthusiasm," Isaac objected. "In a situation like his, anybody would do the same."

"I suppose that's why God brings people into situations like that," Joshua said, sounding almost bored with what must have been a hopeless conversation he'd had with many a Jew before.

"It's hard to believe," Isaac pressed on, "that getting into this Kingdom of God is so easy. Don't you know how hard our Orthodox people strive to please God? When did it become so simple?"

"When the Messiah died," Joshua replied with brevity.

"Oh, stop that Messiah business and call Him Jesus!" You sound like a public relations man." Isaac was genuinely annoyed.

"Well, I'm not the first to call Jesus the Messiah, Isaac. Our prophets did that long ago. He fulfilled our prophecy, you know. That would be very easy to show you."

"Well, if He fulfilled our prophecy, why don't our learned men know it?" Isaac almost sneered.

"Our learned men don't read our prophecy," Joshua explained, never losing the note of patience and sincerity in his voice. "If you decide to spend your life reading the works of men—the laws, the poetry, the traditions—instead of the Book of God, you can make mistakes. I mean our scholars no disrespect, and I know their intentions are good. But personally, when I read prophecy about the mission of the Messiah and His character, and then I read the life of Jesus, I see that they fit together, and that's all there is to that. Anyone will find the same thing."

Isaac was silent, realizing that the missionary was a real professional. A small voice inside him seemed to say more—that the missionary sounded like a man telling the truth. Joshua spoke with the assurance of a man who was totally certain. Isaac had not pictured that when he had been warned about "the tricky missionaries." Knowing that he was losing the debate—if that's what it was—he switched topics.

"Don't you feel strange, walking around in Israel and believing in Jesus?" he asked.

"No, I feel wonderful. I really do. The only difficulty I have comes in watching people who have so little real spiritual power work so hard. I'm frustrated with what I see among our people, and I'm as stymied as Jesus' disciples were as to how to tell them the simple truth about God. When the Messiah returns, then our people will know Him, Isaac. But I wonder how many of us will be left."

Isaac believed him when he said "I feel wonderful." It was obvious; the man was at peace. He was strong, patient, and kind, and Isaac bore him a little envy. He seemed so satisfied, and yet he had a true mission—a calling of God, it seemed to Isaac. How or why God would call a Jew to work for Jesus, he didn't understand, but the fact of the matter was staring at him. Joshua was a *mench*, a human being.

Arriving at the gate, Isaac forced a smile and started to lapse into an appropriate social way of saying thanks and good-bye. But Joshua spoke first, a penetrating look in his eye. His voice was low and firm, as they stood a short distance away from the sentry near the road.

"Two things, Isaac, and listen well. The boy is dead. He died peacefully, and believe me, I *know* he is with God. You did a fine thing today in taking care of him. And he forgivers you and everyone else here. He bears no malice, and he died happy."

Isaac just stared into Joshua's face, dumbfounded.

"The second thing is about Rebecca. She loves you. But you'd better be very careful. She knows what she wants. Make one mistake with her, and you'll lose the best woman you ever knew."

Isaac found his voice and uttered a small,

"But —" when Joshua interrupted, putting his hand firmly on Isaac's shoulder.

"That's all, dear brother," he said quietly but meaningfully. "Call me if you need me. *Shalom*." And he walked away down the road.

In the infirmary room where the boy lay asleep, Rebecca had been resting. After the men left she felt depleted, completely wrung out. She was almost asleep in her chair, looking up every now and then to see that peculiar glow on the boy's peaceful face. While waiting for Isaac to return from taking the missionary to the gate, she hoped that he felt good about Joshua, because she had liked the visitor very much. Even with their religious differences, Rebecca could see a good man—even a great man—in Joshua. He was kind and warm. He was humble and full of the love of God.

The boy spoke quietly, interrupting her thoughts. He said simply, "I'm going to God now."

Rebecca hurried over to his bedside, not feeling the grief for which she had been preparing herself. As she looked into his perfectly serene face, she met the boy's eyes, which shined with what she interpreted as absolute happiness.

She said, "Tell me your name," but it was too late. Without the slightest shift in the expression of peace, the boy's eyes slowly closed. Rebecca was conscious of a new silence in the

room, and she realized that she had been listening for his breathing all day. It was gone
now.

And they hadn't even asked his name.

She took his lifeless hand in her own and
whispered quietly, "Good night, Ishmael."
Then she went back to her chair.

Somehow , the tears wouldn't come. She
had dreaded this inevitable moment when the
boy would slip away; but now that she had
seen it, she only felt peaceful. Her mind began
to talk to God, to thank Him.

At that moment Dr. ben Judah looked up
from his work. Something had cut across his
busy mind; some instinct drew his eyes away
from his papers. He knew the feeling. His patient had died.

Frowning, he tried to remember the circumstances in the room, and he jumped up quickly
when he realized that Rebecca was alone with
the dead boy.

Rebecca did not look up when the doctor
opened the door. She was asleep, he thought.
One glance at the boy confirmed that he was
dead. Dr. ben Judah placed his body between
Rebecca and the bed and woke her gently. "All
right, young lady," he exclaimed cheerily, "it's
time to go. Let's let this patient get a little
rest!"

Rebecca did not object as the doctor hustled her out of the room. "He's asleep. You can check back later on," he was saying.

At the door she faced him and said, "Thank you for all you did for him, Dr. ben Judah," and she quickly walked away.

Dr. ben Judah sighed at the failure of his little ruse. Someday, he hoped, doctors would find a way to just say straightforwardly that a patient had died. Oddly, though, Rebecca did not seem overwhelmed. She had sat with the boy for many hours; the doctor had expected her to weep.

He went back to the little room where the boy lay in the composed stateliness of death. He observed no breathing, but he routinely placed his hand at the side of his patient's throat, assuring himself that all life was gone.

As he did so, a strange feeling came over him. The throat was still, completely dead. There was no pulse, no blood, no warmth. But the face seemed alive! Dr. ben Judah had seen many a cadaver in his long medical experience, but he looked at this boy's face with a new feeling. His brow furrowed and his eyes squinted as he tried to make out what it was that pulled at his mind. Somehow the boy *did* seem just asleep, and not really dead.

This boy had died an extraordinarily peaceful death, the doctor thought, because that glow of peace still remained on the dead face. The doctor thought about the missionary and the peculiar conversation with the boy he'd overheard from his office. That the boy was convinced about his going to God had pleased the doctor. There certainly was no chance whatever that he would recover, but a certain comfort had been provided by the missionary. Speaking medically, the doctor knew the boy would have a better death after that interview.

But this! A corpse with a serene face and a massively injured body! How had this happened?

He felt strange as he pulled up the sheet to cover that victorious face.

While the doctor was phoning the army base, which would send a detail of corpsmen to examine and dispose of the boy's body, Isaac was making his way back to the infirmary. He was still stunned by Joshua's parting messages.

The first seemed like an intelligent guess anyone might have made. Perhaps the missionary was admitting that there was no real healing possible through Christian prayer; perhaps he wanted to seem like some sort of supernatural sage for uttering what might happen anyway before it happened.

But the second message seemed completely beyond the missionary's attempt to assess. Isaac and Rebecca had not said a word to each other—they had barely exchanged a glance—while the missionary was present. If he were just making an assumption, Isaac wished that he wouldn't; the subject was becoming an extremely important one, not to be trifled with. Isaac remembered with confusion the decisive way Joshua had stated, "She loves you." And then he had said, "Make one mistake with her, and you'll lose the best woman you ever knew." How could he characterize people like that, without even really knowing them? How could he say something so personal? He seemed so intelligent and so sensitive otherwise.

Isaac toyed with the notion that the missionary had been perfectly right, and he would find that out eventually. Maybe he did possess a remarkable insight; maybe his closeness to God had something to do with it. He did have some kind of enchanted quality about him, some special charisma that Isaac had responded to, even on the phone.

Isaac was startled to see Rebecca walking toward him some distance from the infirmary. Apparently she had come out to meet him. It could only mean one thing, and Isaac dreaded asking. Rebecca was watching his face as she approached, and Isaac was trying to detect her message. He didn't want to fall into another embrace; he'd had enough of holding Rebecca in response to feelings that came from outside both of them. The next time he held her, he vowed, it would be to express what they felt for each other. *If*, his mind told him, *there was anything to what the "prophet" had said.*

Isaac put his hands in his pockets, in a boyish way of avoiding physical closeness. Rebecca seemed to understand and stopped short of falling into his arms. He expected to see some tears, if the boy had indeed died, or some show of sorrow, but Rebecca seemed very glad about something. Her face fairly shone as she smiled at Isaac.

It occurred to him that he had never really seen her smile before. At least not this way, with real victory on her face. Distrusting his own feelings at the moment, he asked simply, "What happened?"

"He's in paradise," said Rebecca.

Isaac was disconcerted. That was certainly an odd way of putting it. He grew impatient.

"Rebecca, is the boy dead?"

"Yes," she told him. "But he died—happy. Isaac, I wish you'd been there."

Isaac felt very strange about her then. She looked almost glassy-eyed. It wasn't Rebecca, as he knew her. He didn't like this new version of her. It seemed, for one thing, that she was emulating Joshua's style, and doing a bad job of it. Maybe he had misunderstood her, but he didn't care for this "paradise" business. The boy was dead because he had been hit almost directly by a hand grenade and that was the long and short of it. Joshua's assurances of a happy future for his soul, or whatever he meant, and his promises about a new body for the boy, were so much Christian claptrap. That was not the way the Jewish people thought.

Isaac felt the moment had come for him to put his foot down in his relationship with Rebecca. If they were going to continue to see each other, he wanted the terrorist, the missionary, and everything else about this strange incident to fade into the past. And he certainly did not want to hear religious jargon on the subject. Reality was reality. "The Jewish people live" because the Jewish people don't chase rainbows.

He tried to hold those negative thoughts back before he spoke, but she was looking at him in that way again—her eyes seemed to penetrate his brain like searchlights—and he could hide nothing from her.

"You don't see it, do you?" she asked. "You don't see what happened to the boy. Isaac, he left us in peace! Nothing better could have happened."

"I *saw* it, Rebecca. I was there for the service," he carped sarcastically. "But I'm not so sure I believe it all. I'm not so easily hypnotized."

Immediately he wished he could take back his words. He had definitely gone too far. He had insulted her.

He stepped toward her quickly, reaching out with his arms and saying, "Rebecca, it's been a terrible two days. Please forgive me. I didn't mean that."

She evaded his embrace smoothly and proceeded to walk away from him, saying coldly, "I have to be getting back to the nursery now, Isaac. Thank you for all you did."

She was gone, just like that. He stood there, perplexed.

Was that the one mistake already that Joshua had allowed him? She certainly seemed touchy. If this was really love, he didn't think he wanted any.

Isaac made a brief stop at the dining hall. It was already time for supper, and he hadn't had a bite all day. He was quiet and philosophical, sitting alone with his mixed-up thoughts.

He had to see her again, he concluded. At least he had to get her to stand still for an apology. He'd go by the nursery some morning and just talk to her.

With his stomach full and his mind finally empty, he went straight back to his room and his bed. He was bone weary and eager to get back on his work schedule. It was still early evening, but he intended to make up for that short bout with the terrible dreams the night before. He would sleep long and deeply and be up before the sun; he would be the first one to the fields in the morning.

Isaac had doubted that he would dream this night, but he had a wonderful, pleasing dream. He was at some huge wedding—a magnificent marriage supper—in the dream. There were thousands of guests; the happy crowd seemed to go on endlessly. Rebecca was there, and Joshua, too. Perhaps Rebecca was the bride, but Isaac saw no bridegroom. He looked everywhere in the large, decorous room, but he couldn't find the bridegroom anywhere. He supposed that he would find him eventually.

As his eyes swept the faces of the multitude of celebrators, he knew he was waking up and he felt regret. He loved the dream, and he wanted it to go on forever.

The last thing he saw, just before his eyes opened, was the young terrorist, praising God with two good arms lifted high.

SIX

While Isaac was dreaming, Rebecca was making a telephone call to Jerusalem. She shivered in the dark of the hallway of the women's quarters, hoping her father would wake up and answer the phone. It was very late, but she was very excited.

"Shalom," said a weary voice on the distant connection.

"I've found my husband, Papa!" Rebecca exclaimed in a shout.

The rabbi rubbed the sleep from his eyes as best he could and tried to follow his daughter's chatter. She had found a man called Isaac, significantly enough, and as near as he could make out, Isaac was unaware that he was going to be the sacrifice in this case.

Rebecca brought her father up-to-date with the brief, stormy relationship she'd been having on the kibbutz. At first she omitted the part about the missionary, but she became reckless as she exulted in her happiness. She told everything, trusting her father's immense wisdom and his constant prayers for her to marry. She knew he would rejoice.

Rabbi Bethuel tried to get his thoughts to-gether as she went on, knowing that this call as from God. He had entreated the Almighty so many times on behalf of his daughter, preferring her to have married long before this, even in her teens. His family, he feared, would come to an end without Rebecca's marriage; all the relatives had been separated in Europe, and his own wife had passed away after they had settled in Israel.

The rabbi had had a distinguished career as a saboteur in Austria during the war. He and his wife could actually have fled before the Germans came, but instead they had continued to minster to their congregation, and finally to Jews everywhere in hiding places throughout the country.

Using forged ration cards and living in cel-lars, they had helped Jew after Jew escape the Nazis, arranging passage, paying bribes, and cheating the Gestapo out of many Jewish lives. Sometimes they were only minutes ahead of the relentless German police, who could never be satisfied on Jewish blood. Sometimes they confronted a captor head on, and the young, strong rabbi had done what he had to do.

With other agents of the Jewish under-ground, he had blown up trains, stolen weapons and used them, and spirited Jews day and night over the borders of the Third Reich. In addition, he had kept every Passover, and he had said the mourner's *kaddish*, the prayer over the dead, every mourning and every night, realizing that it still was inadequate for the death all around him. He had fought, he had protected his wife, and eventually he had made it to the promised land. Even now, he was regarded as a hero by those who knew him, but he was not satisfied with the tragedy that had been his life.

In truth, the rabbi and his wife had had to live like animals, not heroes. They were the hunted, and they behaved accordingly. Thus,they survived, but they hardly knew each other. It did not breed great love, as outsiders would suppose, for a husband and wife to work together in such dread and for so hopeless a cause. At times they resented each other for having to share the rodents they ate. They avoided marital love for fear of a doomed pregnancy. At the end of the war they could only appreciate each other for their bravery. They were much too exhausted to really live again.

When the war finally stopped, Rabbi Bethuel elected to go to Palestine, as it was then called, even though the borders were closed. He and his wife had suffered on a miserable, pitching, crowded boat across the Mediterranean, only to be turned away at Haifa. Never would he forget the cold and unrelenting face of the British officer, who looked past the mobs of chosen people detained at the dock to tell the crew that the boat would have to depart for holding camps on Cyprus.

On that windy island, his wife contracted the respiratory illness that finally killed her a few years later in Israel. Rebecca, her only child, had never really known her mother.

The rabbi tried to be patient at Cyprus. The Jews were herded into a barbed-wire enclosed camp, which could have been Dachau, except for the lack of gas chambers and ovens. Once when the rabbi was pushed by the rifle butt of a twenty-one-year-old junior officer, he told the youngster in good English, "I've been killing soldiers with my hands for five years. Now touch me again with that gun!" The guard was gone immediately.

When they had finally been permitted to immigrate to Israel, it was only to join another war. In 1948 the rabbi went to the front, which wasn't far from his home, as a captain in the Israeli army. His experience with dynamite came in handy; there weren't enough big guns, and the Jews made do with what they had. On a forgotten Israeli road was an Egyptian armored vehicle Rabbi Bethuel had handled personally. The government had painted it with rust proofer, and it was there to this day, illustrating to the people of Israel what had to be done to reclaim the land. Compared to bombing German trains, it was child's play, thought the rabbi, who was unused to having cover fire and a place to run after the explosion. He was presented a medal which he threw away.

His wife was supposedly assigned as a nurse during that war, but in reality she was given a precious machine gun because she knew how to use it. When Rebecca told her father about the machine gun in the nursery at the kibbutz, he responded with a tired and frustrated shake of his head, and told her that chapter of her mother's life.

When Israel was firmly established after the war, the rabbi had finally resumed his rabbinical duties; but somehow life held little flavor for him, and God seemed very distant. He read in the newspapers about the return of the rabbis to Israel, and how they inspired the Jewish worshipers, but he found it hard to identify with that. Although he was vaguely glad he was still alive, he was so deeply discouraged with his existence that he found it hard to live. He was in his late thirties then, his youthful years having disappeared in a thousand unfair fights, and he now spent his time reading in the holy books and listening to his wife's steady coughing.

How wrong it was, he had told God one day for his wife to suffer so. Why would she be so sick? What had she done to the world to deserve this suffering? He loved her, yes, to the degree that he could care about anything under the circumstances, but she was no longer the woman he had married. What a beautiful girl she had been when he courted her; how modest, how devout, how completely desirable. But now the light was gone from her eyes, and she was a different, unhappy person. She was melancholy all the time, and God well knew that no one could blame her.

First the Nazis had come into her young life. Then the British, and finally the 1948 War. That wasn't life. No one was created to live that way.

He tried to be a husband to her, and in truth they had some deep feelings for each other. They had great difficulty in having pleasure of any kind, though and they may have silently cast blame on each other for their sorrowful lot. When she became pregnant between the early wars, the rabbi rejoiced as best he could, but he feared the childbirth would finish her.

But actually the birth of Rebecca was a new beginning. The first moment the rabbi looked upon his baby daughter, he realized that God was still running the world and the lives of the people in it. What a creation! What a miracle! And mother and baby were both healthy and full of life!

In the next two years the rabbi maintained a real prayer life and communed daily with the Lord. He read deeply in the Law, and he studied the role of fatherhood from the depth of perspective of the Jewish sages. He was kind to his wife, who he saw was steadily failing in health despite the successful birth. He read in the Talmud, "Never make a woman cry; God counts her tears," and he saw to it that his wife never cried again.

He watched as one female personality was slowly forming in his household and one was slowly extinguishing. He listened sadly to his wife as she told him that she realized she was dying. She was hospitalized often, and although the rabbi was thankful for the consummate skill of the Israeli doctors, nothing could be done to save her. In the end she told him to maintain his faith in God—that it was good for him and made a true husband out of him. And she thanked him for her life, for all of his efforts on her behalf.

She held little Rebecca for the last time on a rainy Sabbath day in the hospital. And she cried with her husband that their relationship had to be cut off now, when it was just seeming to bloom. She passed away holding his strong hand.

The rabbi never thought of remarrying but always kept a housekeeper to raise Rebecca and cook for the two of them. He led a small congregation and spent most of his time making a deep study of the Jewish faith from the Law, the Scriptures, and secular history. He lectured Rebecca as she grew, and she was one little girl who understood her Judaism thoroughly. She knew four thousand years of Jewish history and tradition before she went to high school.

Her eventual marriage was important to her father in a deeply personal way. It was a chance for him to relive something. His own marriage had been stopped before it had a proper chance to mature. Rebecca was going to be happy, the rabbi was determined. She would marry a solid Jewish man who respected his faith and knew how to take care of a woman. They would raise sons and daughters of Israel, and the rabbi would rejoice again. The family — who knew where they all were ? — would continue through Rebecca.

Rebecca had seemed to grow up suddenly, in the rabbi's view. One day she was a playful girl, very strong-minded and willful, and then suddenly she was a young woman, subtle and sensitive. He felt as if he had blinked, and there was, a beauty.

Rebecca did not want to go to college but to the land. Her father thought her very sensible; he had never met a successfully educated person who had never worked the soil. After the 1973 War, during which the rabbi was utilized as an intelligence officer and again was decorated (and again he discarded the medal), Rebecca wanted to go north. Like so many young Israelis, she wanted to plant, and she wanted to defend the land.

She worked hard in the hot fields at the kibbutz, but eventually she was put in charge of the nursery. It was her intelligence, her father supposed, that made them see what a good woman she would be with children. But what about that marriage and her own children? Her father had asked more than once if the young men of the kibbutz planted all day and planted all night as well!

Rebecca told him about her feeling of destiny where her man was concerned. He was surely coming soon, she had said on her last trip to Jerusalem. And she was more than ready for him.

She had told her father, "Don't be surprised if I phone you late some night and tell you he has come!"

Well, this was the night, but he *was* surprised.

"Please slow down, Rebecca," requested the sleepy rabbi. "I only get to do this once in life, so let me enjoy it a little."

"Papa, I'm so excited!" she exclaimed, almost out of control.

"Now, that is as it should be," mused the rabbi, "but there are a few details in your story I'd like to ask you about, if I may. First of all, when does the bridegroom get the good news?"

"Well, first he has to come and apologize. We had that little spat. He really is so insensitive. He's going to take a lot of work."

"Rebecca, the way you told me the story, this young man was objecting to your getting so involved with that missionary and his ways. I don't blame him for that. Maybe you should apologize." The rabbi was starting to like Isaac.

"Papa, I'm not turning into a Gentile just because I appreciated the man and what he did!" She stopped short of saying "what he did for the terrorist," because her father's understanding of things did not normally extend to comforting any enemy of the Jews. Rebecca could almost feel his coldness to that part of her story when she told it, and now she was sorry she had given all the details.

"And you're sure this Isaac of yours loves you? If he's still around tomorrow, it will make three days you've known him."

"Papa, you should see the way he looks at me!"

"Never mind, Rebecca. I've seen young men look at you before." Despite his verbalized skepticism, it was easy for the rabbi to see that his daughter was genuinely in love, and he trusted her judgment of what Isaac felt. But he was having an immensely joyous time talking with her, and he didn't want the conversation to end.

"Papa, it will take him a day or two to come around to see me. And when he does, he's going to tell me he loves me. And then I'm going to tell him I love him, too, and we'll be married."

"And will you have the courtship after the wedding, then?" asked the rabbi dryly. "Well, maybe quick marriage is a good idea for you, after all. I know how romantic things are in Galilee. What a beautiful place!"

"Papa!"

This was much more fun for the rabbi than playing games with Rebecca when she was a small child. He cherished every moment. "I love you, Rebecca," he said quickly, so that she would know it yet again and not take offense.

"I love you, too, Papa," she breathed softly. And she blew him a little kiss he could not see.

"Now," said the rabbi after a pause, "may I give you some instructions I'd like you to follow?"

"Of course, Papa."

"Wait for him to come to you, and wait for him to do the asking, please. That's number one! And then, if you haven't scared him off completely, I want you to come and see me here in Jerusalem. I want to tell you some things about the way our people married in the past. I want you to have a real Israeli marriage; that is my fondest wish for you. After I say what I have to say, you and Isaac can make your choice about wedding customs and what you want to do. But at least come and hear me out. I want the best for you."

"Of course, Papa," Rebecca said, almost solemnly. She knew that he would have some lore about ancient tradition to impart to her, and she knew it would be as beautiful as it was impractical. But she would certainly go, and she would surely listen well.

"And you'll wait for *him* to come to *you?*"

"Yes, Papa."

"Don't you go proposing marriage to that man. That's not the way we do things!"

Rebecca only laughed.

"And then you'll come to Jerusalem?"

"To Jerusalem, Papa. I'll be there this week for sure."

"I can't wait to see you, my darling," the rabbi said with a husky voice.

"I love you, Papa," Rebecca said as she hung up the phone.

She stayed a moment by the phone, as if the warmth of her father might still radiate from it after the connection was broken. How joyful he was, and how completely understanding. They had a kind of code they spoke in, Rebecca realized, which could never be explained to anyone else. The words they used had their regular meanings, but behind the words was a feeling, almost a passion, between the two of them. They were an absolutely happy two-member family. Because they understood each other in very special ways, each could feel what the other felt.

Rebecca could picture her father still sitting by the phone, shaking his head and smiling the way he always did when she came up with her special brand of mischief. She knew Isaac would appreciate him deeply, and she hoped that sometime the whole family, including his parents in America, could be together.

Then she smiled as she thought about Isaac. How long would it really take him to come to her? She wondered. A kind of impish light came into her eyes as she thought about the whole world of long looks he had unconsciously given her in the past two days. He had a way of studying her as if she were a specimen of life from another world; he had a longing look that made her want to comfort his loneliness; he had a protective look, where his chin was prominent and his eyes hard as steel; and he had a manly look that embarrassed her every time she saw him watching her. She knew that she could take care of all his needs and everything that his wonderful eyes expressed.

But how long would it take *him* to realize that?

Standing there in the dark, she speculated, at last deciding that Isaac would let one day pass. He would be at the nursery the day after tomorrow, she thought, apologizing for his abrupt manner with her and agreeing that the whole experience with the terrorist and the missionary was God's way to bring them together. By then he would realize that they should not grieve over the boy—he himself would not have wanted that—and that they should think respectfully about Joshua, the missionary. The whole incident was one to be learned from and to be respected as a very special moment of life.

She knew that he was the kind of man who would see things the way she did, and see even more in them than she did.

She could hardly wait for the day after tomorrow!

When Rebecca arrived at the nursery at dawn the next morning, Isaac was waiting for her.

The children had not started to get up yet, and

the lady who spent the night with them was still asleep in the back room. It was very quiet.

They were completely alone, and Rebecca was breathless. She tried hard not to betray her shock or her eagerness at seeing him a day early, by her reckoning. She tried to maintain a normal disposition, even to display a slight coolness toward Isaac. Moving about the room, she began straightening things and getting out some materials for the morning's activities with the children. Isaac sat in a corner which was still not illuminated by the light of the new day. His face was in shadow, but she was determined not to look at him, anyway.

Finally he spoke. "Rebecca, I'm sorry."

If she had had any doubts about him being her man, they were gone now. Her heart was pounding and she barely controlled an urge to rush into his arms. But she knew that wasn't his favorite approach. Isaac was not as impulsive as she, and that was all to the good. Saying nothing, she waited for him to continue.

"It was a very special experience—the whole thing," Isaac said. "I'm sorry the boy died, but I can't help being relieved about how it happened. It was a wonderful experience. I learned something from it."

Isaac waited for Rebecca to speak, but again she said nothing. He had awakened with something special in his mind this beautiful morning. His magnificent dream of the marriage supper, his realization of the wonder of Rebecca and everything that had happened—he wasn't going to let any more time go by before he found out if she felt anything for him. He had even gone so far in his wishful thinking as to picture to two of them marrying someday. He wanted a wife like her, a woman who would fill his heart and his mind every time she came near him. But first he had to take a certain plunge, for better or worse, and he did so immediately.

"Rebecca, I love you," he said softly.

She stopped what she was doing and stood perfectly still. Then she came slowly over to him and stood in front of his chair. Her face was extremely serious, almost severe. She looked down at him. "How much do you love me?" she asked in a small whisper.

What did she mean? His mind raced. He didn't dare hope—But what did she mean? She was standing before him like an offering, as if to say, "Make yourself clear. What do you want?" He swallowed and tried to compose himself. Only one thought screamed through his mind, and he couldn't get away from it. He blurted it out.

"Rebecca, marry me!"

He leaped up and seized her in his arms, practically crushing her slender form. He felt crazy, and the words he had said seemed to have come from somewhere else. Was he proposing marriage just like that? What would she think of him? What would she say?

Then he became conscious of the fact that she was holding him as desperately as he was holding her. She hadn't jumped away. She didn't start laughing, and she didn't seem shocked. He waited a painfully long time before she spoke.

Of all of the richness of the Hebrew tongue, Rebecca chose the two words Isaac wanted to hear the most: *"Kehn Yitzchak,"* "Yes, Isaac."

He held her even more tightly for a long moment, and she returned his fervor, clinging to him joyfully. Then he shouted, "Marry me, Rebecca!"

She shouted back, "Yes, Isaac!" then they both broke into gales of laughter.

There were stirring noises in the next room now and Isaac and Rebecca crushed their laughter into small giggles. They still clung together, hoping it would be a while before anyone entered the room.

Rebecca said softly, "Will you please kiss me now? Do I have to tell you everything?"

Isaac kissed her tenderly, savoring their frenetic excitement mixed with the solemn commitment they had both just made. She clung to his lips, her eyes closed tightly. As soon as the kiss was over, she said, "Now kiss me again." There was something in her eyes now - very demanding and passionate. Isaac kissed her deeply. She broke off the kiss very quickly, breathlessly exclaiming, "Isaac, I love you so much!"

"Come outside," he urged, wanting to talk more before the children came into the front room. Taking his hand, she followed him out.

Outside they stood near the rocket sculpture in the early morning light and laughed some more. "What are we doing?" Isaac said.

"We're getting married, husband," said Rebecca, with a twinkle in her eye. Then she was serious. "We really are getting married, Isaac. I will be your wife." She lowered her eyes. "I've never been with a man. I've never loved anyone else." She felt a certain shyness, for from some instinct within her she wondered if he was confident about her—if she would really be a good wife for him. Perhaps he would have wanted a woman with more knowledge of men, more experience with them.

But he calmed her fears with his quiet statement, "Then we'll both be starting from the beginning."

Tears stung her eyes as she looked up at him. "Will you pray, Isaac?" she asked, referring to her man as all Orthodox women did.

Taking her hands, he held them as he prayed very simply, "Dear God of Israel, bless our marriage."

The lights came on in the nursery behind them as they looked up from their prayer. "I really have to go, Isaac," she said. "Darling, may I go to Jerusalem right away to tell my father? May I go today? I promised him I would."

Isaac wasn't accustomed to making such decisions. In fact, he wasn't used to anyone asking, "May I?" He was starting to like married life already. "Of course you can. You can go today. Can you be back sometime tomorrow?"

"Yes, darling. Thank you." She pulled away from him to go into the nursery. "I'll be back as soon as possible. Tomorrow for sure. I love you." And with that she disappeared into the nursery.

Isaac stood still, as if in shock. That had been a very fast, extremely dramatic meeting with Rebecca, he agreed with himself. He had made a marriage proposal. Well, fine. That's what he wanted, he thought.

Dual voices kept sounding in his head as he went toward the fields. A discussion was going on about that extraordinary moment when he realized he wanted Rebecca completely. One voice seemed to say that things were happening too fast, but another seemed calmer and very satisfied. On the whole, Isaac agreed with the latter.

He was glad she would be gone for the day, because he had a lot of private thoughts, to say the least. He wondered why she didn't just phone her father and give him the news; but then, she had said she had promised him she'd come.

He stopped walking for a moment and concentrated on something that was bothering the back of his mind. She said she had promised her father she would come to Jerusalem, as if she had made that promise recently. What in the world did she mean by that? Was she just going to drop in on her father and say, "Hi, I'm getting married'? Had she somehow suspected that she was going to be getting married?

Turning on his heel, he headed back toward the nursery. He was going to find out who had outsmarted whom.

Rebecca looked up as if she was expecting him. As soon as he opened the door, she smiled that mischievous smile that went right to the softest spot in his heart. The children were already in the room, playing with the toys Rebecca had gotten out earlier.

"I said too much, didn't I?" she asked. He could see that her face was still flushed from their embraces.

"Yes, I think you said too much, wife." He paused and then asked her, in a manner of a detective, "Did you call your father last night?"

Ignoring the question, she pretended to be busy with one of the children. She practically snatched up a baby who was engrossed in turning the pages of a coloring book.

"Did you call your father last night and tell him I was about to propose to you?"

"Kehn, Yitzchak," she said sweetly.

He was speechless. "I love you," he finally said.

"And I love you, too, Isaac. Now go away and let me work!"

SEVEN

By noon of that same incredible day, Rebecca was at the bus depot in Tiberias. It was the third day in a row she had asked to be released from her work, and this time the *mazkir* was really impressed. "Something seems to happen to you every day," he said in Yiddish as he granted the leave for Rebecca to tell her father about impending marriage.

Rebecca had always loved this bus trip through the Jordan River valley. The prophet Isaiah had said that someday the Israeli desert would blossom like a rose, and surely these lush green fields fulfilled his vision. The ride through the farmland, with its impressive irrigation machinery and tall rows of corn, never failed to make her proud of her people and thankful to God. Who but the Jews, with God, could make these dry fields yield such nourishment for the body and the soul?

She had taken the alternate route to Jerusalem, through the mountainous terrain of Samaria, on several occasions, but there the hand of God was not so clearly seen. Passing through

Nazareth and the other hot, sleepy little towns where Arabs ran trinket shops for tourists, Rebecca was never as inspired. The withered, forbidding Samaritan soil gave up sustenance only for the Bedouin, the nomadic desert people who inexplicably wandered from place to grudging place, calling the sand their home. Rebecca always shuddered when she saw the Bedouin children, scrawny and hungry-eyed, trudging along with baby goats for their playmates, and heavy garments for their shelter from the heartless desert sun.

As the bus made its way southward through the valley, the vegetarian grew more space. The farther from the Sea of Galilee, the less life on the land, and Rebecca waited eagerly for the pleasant sight of green Jericho, an oasis of palms and breezes on the way to the Dead Sea.

Jericho was an Arab town, too, but here the people were more animated. There were shade, water, and pretty little homes, and for thousands of years the wanderers from the thankless Dead Sea territories had caught their breath at the very sight of this peaceful village. From time immemorial, Jericho meant a drink of cool water. The bus stopped momentarily to pick up a few soldiers and an Arab businessman heading for Jerusalem. Rebecca remained in her seat, savoring the eastern breezes through her open window. Thinking about the time when her ancestors of the wilderness had come into Israel at this place, she realized that they must have loved their first sight of the promised land when they blew their trumpets around the city's walls.

The bus then headed west into the mountains for the long climb to Jerusalem. The Holy City lay high in the hills of Judah, and the old, British-made bus strained with all it had, illustrating the difficulty of coming to God at His citadel. How many devout Jewish pilgrims had climbed these hills on foot to commemorate the holy feasts at the Temple of God through the millennia past? Rebecca reflected. Truthfully, she would not have wanted to live in the days of the Temples, when the physical life was put to such agonies in the attempt to sanctify the spiritual life. How faithful they were, the ancient Jews, she thought. How little credit anybody, even the Jews, gives today to those hearty worshippers from the distant past who sacrificed themselves, as well as the best of their possession, to give the world its only accurate concept of God.

Bethlehem came into view then, with its remarkable collection of polyglot churches and its berobed priests of every sliver of belief in Jesus. What would the Israeli Prophet born here say if He saw the place today? Rebecca wondered. Had he not taught so simple a message of belief in God and sacrifice of self? How amazed He would be, Rebecca thought, to see this motley variety of clergy and believers, shifting inevitably with the times. And how furious the Galilean might be, in view of His objection to the animal sellers in the Temple, to see what profiteering went on at the very site of His birth. Bethlehem, Rebecca thought, could cause some people to lose their faith altogether.

But now her thoughts turned to Jerusalem, just ahead. The bus would wind its way past Bethany, the little hamlet to the east of the Old City, where Lazarus was reputedly raised from the dead, and then push on into Jerusalem and the bus station, where Rabbi Bethuel would be waiting to take her in his arms.

How she ached to see her father again! It had been months since her last visit, and try as she might, Rebecca never felt fully like an adult. She was his little girl. She was still a member of her father's family, and his home was still her home. And besides, with the exception of Isaac, for whom she felt so overwhelming a passion, her father was the only man she really loved in this world.

As the bus made its way through crowded Jerusalem into the New City, she nearly jumped up and down on her seat with anticipation. He would be waiting at the platform in the station, a strong, broad man with a bushy, black beard only recently showing white around the edges. He would be wearing his black hat, and his small, kind eyes would be peering through his rimless spectacles, searching the crowd for his only daughter. The prophets Isaiah and Daniel must have looked like her father, Rebecca always thought.

How joyous an occasion this meeting was going to be!

Rebecca was not disappointed. Her father smothered her in a wonderful bear hug at the busy bus station and couldn't seem to stop kissing her as they stood on the platform. With all of the bustling crowds brushing by, going to and from the rickety old buses, and all of the normal pandemonium of an Israeli public place, Rebecca could still, with teary eyes, feel warm in her father's strong arms.

After exchanging their usual love words, they decided to walk around about three miles to her father's small apartment in the downtown New City section. As they strolled, they held hands like lovers. Rebecca was still wide-eyed at the frenzied activities of the streets of her beloved Jerusalem, though she had grown up here in the midst of the magnificent turmoil. Galilee was never like this, she thought, and neither, she was sure, was any other replace on earth.

They passed through that singular concoction of the very new and very old that is the architecture of God's city today; high-rise apartment buildings stood by stone enclosures that might have housed biblical personalities, for all anyone knew. Roman styling, deteriorated with age but still obvious, graced buildings standing by modern supermarkets and movie theaters.

Rebecca could not help but notice the plain dress of the people. Most of them used clothing designed for long wear; the young people favored blue jeans, and the older people wore outdated wool pants and dresses. Few of Jerusalem's populace had the money to dress according to fashion anymore. Only the tourists and an occasional businessman passing by seemed to be wearing clothing chosen for appearance. The Israelis, due to the inflation that had prevailed since the 1973 War, had funds for little else than rent and food. But they wore their plainness well, Rebecca sensed, uncomplaining of the hardships of founding a new nation.

As they passed near the *Mea Shearim*, the Orthodox sector of Jerusalem, Rebecca began to see the women wearing *sheitelim*, wigs. Wives of the strictly orthodox Jews shaved their heads as an act of submission to their husband, and they wore short, curly wigs and fancy hats in the streets. Rebecca had once been told that this custom prevented the Orthodox woman from ever running off with another man—the would-be adulterer would be turned off by the bald head. Rebecca almost shuddered thinking of the difficulty of their law; it certainly wasn't for her.

The Orthodox were almost belligerent about their faith. Some of them refused to use Israeli money, holding that the present land of Israel was invalid since the Messiah had not yet come to establish it. In their zeal to maintain the purity of the chosen people against the Messiah's soon coming, they went around Jerusalem with black marking pens, blotting out movie ads which showed people kissing. They substituted the letter *T* for the plus mark in arithmetic classes in order never to have to draw a cross of any kind; this expressed their distaste with the false Messiah from Nazareth. They were proud men, each outdoing the other in the slenderness of the robes he wore and the piety with which he approached the God of Israel. But Rebecca was glad that her father, whose sincerity toward God was exceeded by no one else's as far as she could discern, had not opted for such holy trappings. He chose simple clothing, usually black, that more or less reflected his commitment without being overbearing.

As they progressed down the Jaffa Road toward the heart of the city, things became busier and more modern. It was as if they had stepped forward a few centuries; the young women here wore jewelry and high heels and dramatic makeup, all set off by the inevitable blue jeans. They would cuff the jeans to the knee for "evening wear," Rebecca knew. Far from wearing wigs, the Sabra girls let their black hair hang long and free. They were beautiful and graceful, thought Rebecca, who as an adolescent had been envious of their dark-eyed good looks. Her own more European-like features—soft brown hair, light complexion, less prominent cheekbones—had always seemed somehow inferior, even less godly, against these more pure women of the land.

She had always felt somewhat inferior to them in her frailty as well. Police cars passed, with young women officers looking over the crowds as they walked along, and Rebecca knew that these policewomen commanded real respect in Jerusalem. Some of them went on to become valued army officers, filling vital support roles when the nation saw combat, as it did so often. Rebecca pitied the occasional male tourist—usually American—who tried to "make time" with one of these uniformed girls in the streets. He usually got the shock of his young life!

As they passed in front of the King David Hotel, where rich tourists from the West congregated at all times of the year, Rebecca tried not to notice the tourists' swaggering ways and their loudness in the entranceway of the plush hotel. Israel needed their contribution, and while few natives of the land appreciated their mannerisms, they were tolerated for their generous ways with money. And after all, they were Jews, with a God-given right to their homeland. If they only chose to visit occasionally instead of to live in the land, that was their affair. They were still "at home" in Israel as in no other country in the world.

Rebecca had always smiled at the little sign

that graced the entrance of the small cafe called "Goliath's," across the street from the hotel. The advertisement said, "Just a stone's throw from the King David."

They occasionally passed religious people in Indian saris and other Eastern costumes. There were gurus in Israel, trying to convert the Jews to the ways of the mysterious East, even as they had appealed to King Solomon. There were Hare Krishnas in the streets, "Moonies" from the cult of the Korean Reverend Moon, and the inevitable Christian evangelists. The latter did their dangerous work more quietly, being the most despised among the many proselytizers in Israel. Public messages about conversion to Jesus had caused the government to cancel the visas of some Christians—they were virtually deported—while the representatives of other religions seemed to be able to move about more freely.

The varied architecture of the Holy City was graced by an equal variety of nature itself. Ancient olive trees were prevalent in the city, and biblical flora grew in backyards everywhere. What God had planted still grew here.

The people also seemed selected out of myriad times and cultures, as if to match their landscape. Arab street vendors plied the trades of their ancestors of thousands of years gone by, and snappily dressed businessmen strode through groups of shirt-sleeved tourists speaking sundry languages. It was a kind of carnival of history; in the variety of faces to be seen on the downtown streets, one could almost study all of humanity from its very roots to the present day. Here and there could be seen secular Orientals, middle Eastern natives of every racial connection, black Africans, Europeans, Americans, Jewish emigrants from Russian and India—it simply went on and on, the Jerusalem "people's show," running almost continuously since King David.

Rebecca was amazed, as always, and a little fearful. She clung to her father's firm arm, nothing with approval the obvious presence of plenty of Israeli police and military personnel in the crowds. Her father spoke to her now and again, asking questions about the kibbutz and the situation in the north generally; but mostly they watched the incredible entertainment of the streets, the rabbi perceiving that his daughter would be more fascinated after her absence.

Apart from the excitement of the streets caused by the sights and sounds, there was also an ever present danger. Not many days before, a bomb had been set off by a terrorist in Zion Square, the busiest downtown intersection, when crushes of people were parading down the sidewalks and auto traffic was heavy. The rabbi had rushed from his nearby flat to care spiritually for the wounded, but he was not at all prepared for the hideous, butcher-shop scene at the epicenter of the explosion. A group of young people, some tourists and some natives, had been shopping in a small boutique near the bomb. Pieces of human flesh and bones were found amid the debris on the opposite sidewalk after the blast. Furious, rabbi Bethuel had rejected the idea of offering prayers and instead showed his army identification to the police wading through the crowds. He was determined to ferret out the vermin who had done this inhuman act, but he paid the price emotionally. For a week he remained physically sick for awakening a part of himself that he had put aside with difficulty earlier in his life. The rabbi no longer wanted to hunt men.

As always, Rebecca was delighted to see her father's immaculate apartment. The three rooms were laid out for study, with everything—scrolls, books of the Law, notebooks, tape recorders—in its proper place. He was a meticulously disciplined man, whose hunger for knowledge about his people knew no end. He studied competently in several languages and even had contributed translation of ancient documents from biblical Hebrew and Aramaic. A self-taught scholar of ancient history and tradition, he was sought after by the best minds both in Israel and abroad, on the subject of his people, and in wartime as an intelligence agent, on the psychology of the Arab bearing arms. He was a thinker to be reckoned with, a man of real accomplishment.

Only when Rebecca was seated and supplied with a tall glass of fruit juice did her father broach the subject of her impending marriage. He was his usual subtle, twinkle-eyed self. "I assume by your early arrival that the fox has stepped into the trap."

Rebecca had only had time to tell him when the bus would get in when she phoned earlier from Tiberias, for numbers of people had been waiting to use the one telephone. But she knew he had been able to trace the success of her venture in her voice. Having planned to wait until he asked questions, she had mastered herself well. But now she began to gush forth the wonders of Isaac and the miracle of their meetings and falling in love.

The rabbi listened as Rebecca went on and on through the story of Isaac's brief but effective courtship—how brave he was, how intelligent, how exactly attuned to her. Stroking his beard absently now and then, the jabbering girl's father listened only for the genuineness of the man he was hearing about, and he was more than satisfied as Rebecca finally ran down to a stopping point. He had been thoroughly brought up-to-date, just as though he had been at the kibbutz for the remarkable past three days.

"All right, child," he said when she had concluded. "I wanted you to come here so that I could give you some instruction on how to get married."

Rebecca looked at him strangely, but she was ready for anything.

"I told you that our people had a marriage tradition that was very beautiful, very godly. It was the tradition of Israel when we were last here in our land, in the first century. And while I'm not going to insist that you have a two-thousand-year-old wedding ceremony, I did want you to hear about it. I hope you will go back and tell your Isaac what I said and see if he wants to marry like a real Israeli."

Rebecca wondered if this last remark were not a slight slur on Americans in general, for whom the rabbi spared little real love. In any case, she knew that when the rabbi saw Isaac, he would see an Israeli in the man. As she herself understood Americans, Isaac was not one of them. At least he had an instinct for work, for sweat, and for fighting; he knew how to commit himself to his country and to help build it; that much was certain in her mind.

"People didn't exactly 'fall in love' in the old days," the rabbi began, his eyes suddenly filled with his mental images of Israel in all its ancient glory. "Marriages were more normally set up and executed according to a plan that fit the needs of the whole society of Jews.

"When a young man saw the girl he wanted—and like your Isaac, it didn't take him long to figure out—he consulted with his father about the idea of marrying her. Sometimes his father picked the girl, and no consultations were necessary. In any case, when the bridegroom's father approved of the choice, the young man would go to the bride's house and speak with her father. Let me tell you, fathers used to really count for something in Israel!"

Rebecca nodded politely, but she wanted to kiss him instead. Did he suppose he didn't count with her?

"At the bride's house," the rabbi went on, "the young man would do three very important things in connection with their wedding. He would make a covenant with the bride—an actual contract; he would drink a cup of wine with her, which sealed the covenant; and finally, he would pay a price for her. Her father would be entitled to money for his daughter."

"So, you're going to turn me into a profit!" Rebecca exclaimed with a smile. "I could tell you had something up your sleeve. How much do you think I'll bring?"

"Now, daughter, let me tell you something. The customs of our people deserve a little bit of respect, even from the modern generation." He was serious, Rebecca could see, without meaning to berate her. "The bride price had its good points. A young man had to be very serious about getting married, because he had to make a sacrifice. And in the olden times a man with a daughter had suffered financially bringing her up; after all, she was not the field worker that a son would have been."

"But I've worked for you all these years," Rebecca protested, with a gleam in her eye. "I've cooked and cleaned for you, and listened to all your old stories about Israel. I practically raised you! Maybe you should be paying *me!*"

"Oh, Rebecca, Rebecca. What a girl! I think the one to be paid should be Isaac. I wonder if he knows what he's getting into." The rabbi was filled with joy over his daughter's alert mind and good humor. Resolutely, he pressed on with his explanation of the matrimonial customs of ancient Israel.

"Now, after the groom had made the covenant, drunk the cup, and paid the price, he would make a little speech to the bride. You see, he was going to leave her for a long time and go back to his father's house. He was going to build a bridal chamber for her, a place where they would have their first coming together in marriage—what you call the honeymoon today. And before he left, he would tell her, 'I go to prepare a place for you.'"

"He would leave her at a time like that?" Rebecca asked in astonishment. "After making a contract and drinking the wine and paying the price? Father, that's disappointing."

"The bride didn't worry, Rebecca. That was the point of the contract and the cup—and even the money. Don't worry, the young man would always return, no matter how long it took him to build the bridal chamber. He had *paid* for his bride, and he was certainly going to collect what he had paid for. Our people have never been careless with money, you must admit."

"How long would he stay away?" Rebecca asked, fearing the worst.

"A long time, by any bride's standards," the rabbi answered, smiling at her. "He would have to finish the chamber and have it approved by his father. It had to be stocked with provisions—the bride and groom were going to remain inside for seven days, which was the prescribed length of the old-time 'honeymoon.' And it had to be beautiful—she wouldn't want to greet her new husband just anyplace, after all. It took quite a bit of work on the part of the groom to build a first-class bridal chamber. And it had to be right to win his father's approval. If anyone asked the bridegroom, during the year or so that he was engaged in the building process, when he would be getting married, he would say, 'I don't know. Only my father knows.' And sure enough, he could not go back and claim his bride until his father approved the chamber and said that the time was right."

"I'm getting a little bit suspicious, Father," Rebecca said with a cautious smile. "It sounds like a lot of waiting around to me. What bride would want to wait a year?"

"A bride who wanted to be sure she was loved," the rabbi declared. "A bride who wanted to know that her young man would pay for her in money and in work. Believe me, the Jewish girls of ancient times knew they were loved, and for a woman to know she is loved is heaven on earth for her!"

"All right," sighed Rebecca. "That's very beautiful. But what would she be doing all this time? A year is a long time to wait!"

"Well, she waited, and she waited with dignity. She would wear her veil whenever she went out, in order that some other young man wouldn't try to initiate a contract with her. Now she was called, 'set apart,' 'consecrated,' 'bought with a price.' In effect, she was no longer her own person, but an individual contracted to her bridegroom. She conducted herself with due respect for her agreement with the groom. Certainly she never kept company with any other young man, and she used her time to think about married life and to prepare herself for it. As she gathered her trousseau, she always waited, being home every night, especially as the time went on. She certainly didn't want to be caught away from home when the bridegroom came. The tradition was that he would come at night, even at midnight, and try to take her by surprise."

"What a pleasant surprise," Rebecca mused, dreaming of being taken away in the night by a handsome bridegroom to a beautiful, far-off bridal chamber.

As if reading her mind, the rabbi went on. "Yes, it was an 'abduction.' The Jewish brides were 'stolen' out of their houses. The bride would be waiting with her bridesmaids and her sisters and whoever she wanted to take in the wedding party with her and they would all have oil in their lamps in case the groom did choose to come at night. As the time went on, they were ready to go every night. And suddenly, one night the bridegroom would come. The bride's father and brothers would look the other way, as long as it was the young man with the contract," the rabbi smiled, "and the bride and her friends would be whisked off into the night."

"But, Father, a girl can't be ready every minute to go on a trip. Didn't she have a *little* bit of warning?"

"Well, she did, as a matter of fact. The custom was that when the groom's party was close enough to the home of the bride to be heard, they would shout; and when the bride heard the shout, she knew she was as good as married!"

"Well, thank heaven for that shout. I'd hate to be caught with cold cream on my face," Rebecca replied. "Did the young men really rush in and just seize her?"

"Absolutely. They just grabbed every girl in sight, making doubly sure to get the one wearing the veil. The bride would have her veil ready, since the party was going to go through the streets and she was still not married."

Rebecca almost shuddered at the delicious-ness of the ancient custom. How romantic were the chosen people, she thought. How clever at life. "Then what happened?" she asked, eager to follow the lovely story to its promised con-clusion—a magnificent wedding.

"Well, the young men would head toward the groom's father's house with the bride and her friends. They would travel through the streets, making quite a bit of noise with their laughing. You know, nowadays we know there's a wedding when we see decorated cars. Well, they knew there was a wedding in the old days when they heard those young peo-ple laughing their way through the night. But if strangers looked out, they wouldn't know who the bride was because of the veil. People not concerned with this particular wedding—those who were not members of the family—just wouldn't be in on who that bride was."

"And then they would go to the bridal cham-ber," Rebecca said, her voice glowing as she urged her father on.

"Yes, the bride and her groom would go into the chamber while the wedding party waited outside. There would also be a large crowd of wedding guests—friends of the groom's father—assembled at the house, awaiting the couple. Everyone would wait until the bride-groom would tell a trusted friend through the door that the marriage was consummated. Then the celebrating would start."

"He would announce that the marriage was consummated!" repeated Rebecca with some embarrassment. "That seems very personal."

"Well, that's just the exactitude of the chosen people, daughter," the rabbi said, sitting back in his chair and exulting with the very joy of the tradition. "They never had any annulments, and every marriage was started right, in its proper place at the proper time. Our people did not snicker at the sanctified relations between husband and wife. Instead, the Jews honored this gift of God. They merely were certain that they were celebrating an accomplished marriage."

Rebecca nodded, unable to deny the logic of it. She knew that she would be shy at such proceedings, but she knew her father well enough to know that he just delighted in telling her the tradition. He would never insist that she follow it to the letter.

"So the people would be waiting outside the chamber," the rabbi continued, "until they knew that the bride and groom were husband and wife. The next time they would see the bride, at the end of the seven days, she would have her veil off and would be a wife, not a bride. They would spend the entire time celebrating the grand occasion, if this were really a proper Jewish wedding. They would go on for seven days. It was like having jury duty to be invited to one of those old weddings. Sometimes they would run out of wine and have to get more; it was hard to plan for so many people for so long a time."

Rebecca, overwhelmed by the sheer beauty of the tradition, had a small wish in her heart that she and Isaac could fulfill it, at least symbolically. She would talk to him about that, she promised herself, feeling sure he would appreciate the loveliness of the custom.

"At the end of the seven days of celebration," her father continued, "the bride and groom would come out, now husband and wife. And then there would be a grand marriage supper—what we now call the reception. Everyone would congratulate the new couple, and it would be a scene of wonderful joy. And finally the new couple would leave to take up residence in the husband's house. He would have prepared a place for them to live, his own 'kingdom,' as it were, and the couple would go there, leaving his father's house. They would permanently reside there, with the husband hoping they wouldn't have too many daughters and have to go through all that with each one!"

Rebecca jumped up and threw herself onto her father's lap, hugging him with laughter and even a few tears. She kissed his cheek softly, nestling her face against his beard, and said, "I'm so glad you told me all that. I feel married already. What an inspiration! How wonderful it must be to know all about the Jewish people!"

EIGHT

At the bus station the next morning, Rebecca solemnly promised her father that Isaac would learn of the beautiful ancient wedding custom and that they would try to honor it however they could. The rabbi was satisfied. He had probably used the whole thing as an excuse to share his daughter's happiness, Rebecca thought.

They had walked through the streets again, all the way to the station, and they had laughed together as though they were both children. They had slept well and had drunk deeply of their very special love relationship. It was a lovely morning.

Just before Rebecca boarded her bus, the rabbi extracted a promise that Isaac would be presented in Jerusalem as soon as possible. "He owes me at least a look at him, if not some cash," the father of the bride admonished. As he kissed her in the doorway of the bus, he had tears on his cheeks, running into his beard.

Rebecca rode along, barely conscious of the scenery of the Holy Land this time, being completely swept away with the two wonderful loves of her life—her father and her bridegroom. She wouldn't trade places with any woman anywhere, she thought. She was in a total reverie for almost all of the three-hour trip.

Only the grim reality of the electrified cyclone fences that marked the border with Jordan intruded into her feeling of pleasure. As the bus made its way through the valley, it passed close to this tense division of property which had been contested since the time of Joshua, if not since Abraham before him. She had noted the comforting presence of a redheaded soldier in the Jerusalem bus station. Now he sat a few seats behind her, his rifle beside him. The omnipresent Israeli army, a necessity of life in the promised land, had been a part of Rebecca's memory since her infancy.

By the time green Galilee was in view and the bus was passing by the sea, Rebecca was asleep in her seat. She longed for a quick trip back to the kibbutz and Isaac's arms. She would be arriving during his afternoon break, and she was sure he would be close to the nursery. When he had ordered her to be back in one day, she had shivered with delight. And she had done what he said. He would be waiting.

But a shock awaited her at the end of the trip in Tiberias. As she debarked from the bus, a tall, blond man took her arm smoothly and said in her, "This way, Rebecca." She knew he was a policeman of some sort, perhaps a government agent. They all looked so blond and non-Israeli that they were unmistakable.

She resisted him reflexively, trying to pull away, but he had taken her arm firmly and would not let go. Instead, he gave her arm a squeeze to indicate that he meant business. At the same moment the redheaded soldier from the bus was standing besides her, taking her small bag from her other hand and saying, "Please go along quietly, Miss. Just routine."

Rebecca was astounded. Obviously the soldier had been following her on the bus. Perhaps he had followed her in Jerusalem as well. But what had she done?

The blond man was courteous but definite as he said, "This way, please," and took her with a firm grip to a car parked in a bus lane. It was not a police car, and Rebecca had sudden fears of a genuine abduction. Stopping in her tracks, she demanded identification of the blond man. He said, "Into the car, please," and nearly shoved her through the rear door, which was held open by the soldier. The blond man got in beside her, while the soldier got behind the wheel. Rebecca swallowed hard and wondered if she should scream.

But suddenly the blond man was holding a card, which she immediately recognized, in front of her eyes. He was a government security officer—in effect, a secret agent of some importance. He was apologizing for any discourtesy to Rebecca in the station, and he repeated again that meaningless but somehow terrifying statement, "Just routine."

Rebecca asked him again what this was all about, but she received no answer. The agent looked at her with something like sympathy, as if to say, "This is a matter I have no control of; just relax," but he said nothing. Rebecca sat back, relieved to notice that the soldier was not trying to speed away from Tiberias but was heading directly into the heart of the town.

At about the same time Isaac was in a similar situation.

He had come in from the fields and eaten his lunch, intending to maintain a vigil at the nursery for the afternoon, but he was asked to report to the *maskir's* office. There he and the *mazkir* were joined by Dr. ben Judah as an agent and a car stood by. The driver, the agent, and the three men from the kibbutz were then driven into Tiberias.

An hour or so later, all the parties came together at a small building which adjoined the back of the Tiberias police station. Rebecca was greatly relieved to see Isaac enter, along with the doctor and the muchtar, her friends. Since arriving a few moments earlier, she had sat in silence on a hard bench between her two escorts.

The benches were lined up facing a desk at the front of the room, a facility which obviously served as a courtroom. Rebecca looked quizzically back at Isaac, who had been seated in a row behind her, but he only shrugged at her and made a kiss with his lips. She smiled for the first time since her disconcerting arrival in Tiberias.

The various escorts sat quietly, saying nothing, apparently waiting for something. At length, a door opened and a chubby, smiling, friendly faced man with a bushy, black moustache entered the room. Sitting down heavily at the desk, he said, "Forgive me, forgive me, one and all. I'm really terribly sorry to receive you under such mysterious conditions."

At that, a uniformed policeman entered the same door, handcuffed to Joshua. They were seated on the front bench.

"Oh, please take those handcuffs off that man!" the chubby man at the desk exclaimed immediately. "These people have had enough cops and robbers for one morning."

Rebecca could not help but smile at the harried man at the front desk, who looked very embarrassed at all of the proceedings. He smiled back, and even shrugged his shoulders as if to indicate, "What can I do? It's my job."

Then he leaned forward and started explaining. "First, my name is Inspector Joseph Cohen, and again I apologize for all this nonsense. Please consider yourself my guests, and please know that I am honored by the presence of each of you. There is a matter of routine investigation that I must pursue this morning; and after I set my mind at rest, I'm sure you'll all be free to go."

All parties present studied the inspector and waited for further explanation. The agents in the room, looking as though they had been through the same scene many times before, stared absently off into the corners of the room and at the floor. It was certain, however, that they were alert to anyone who might suddenly try to break out. They obviously had been ordered to remain among the inspector's "guests," and they knew their work. Isaac was thinking that something really important was about to happen and he didn't understand a bit of it. Rebecca was beginning to relax, taking an instinctive liking to the inspector. The *mazkir* was impassive. Dr. ben Judah looked bored and occasionally turned in his seat to look at the agents and the other parties in this mysterious situation. His face was frozen in a most disapproving expression. Joshua, who had apparently been there before them, was calm.

The inspector went on: "It just bothers me— the thing that happened this week. I have a terrorist raid on a kibbutz. OK, that happens. My men are always there and always ready. But this time one assailant gets through to the main compound. And he's just a boy, this one, but he somehow gets through. This boy heads for the nursery—or maybe he doesn't know just where he's heading—but anyway, he almost gets there. The closest people to him before the grenade hits are here in this room—you two, Isaac and Rebecca."

Isaac and Rebecca remained silent. Trying to see what the inspector was getting at. Isaac thought that if he or Rebecca were going to be accused of complicity with the terrorist, he would lose all faith in the Israeli secret service.

Seeming to catch Isaac's look, the inspector said kindly, "Now, please just let me go on. Something is disturbing me about this situation, and I want to spell it all out. Would anyone like coffee?"

Everyone just shook their heads at this unexpected offer, impatient to hear what else the inspector had to say. This was not the time for a coffee break.

"All right," the inspector continued, with a smile that Rebecca was now beginning to dislike. "The boy is badly wounded and is taken to the infirmary. Dr. ben Judah here treats him as best he can, but the injuries are too severe. There is no hope for our young Palestinian friend.

"But he is not left alone to die. He has visitors, and a curious combination of them, at that. The young lady from the nursery is the first to arrive. Then the field worker, Isaac, who covered the assailant's position on the roof but never fired at him. And finally, we have our devout Christian friend here," the inspector said with almost a curl to his lip, "who is the most surprising visitor of all. This is a very popular terrorist, you all must admit.

"Now, then, the boy dies, as expected. Isaac

walks our distraught missionary to the kibbutz gate and has a confidential conversation with him before he departs. Then he visits Rebecca for more confidential conversation. Everybody seems to be whispering in everybody else's ear."

Isaac began to think that this perfectly crazy inspector was going to convict them all of something or other. *They're always watching everybody,* he thought. *How can we live this way?* In truth, he was utterly disgusted by the whole idea of government agents observing his movements on a kibbutz. But then it occurred to him that he had very definitely asked for all this when he had decided to come to Israel. When in the long history of this tragic nation had its people been able to trust *anybody*, even each other? No, he would be patient with the inspector and his staff of clandestine observers. In the final analysis, his life depended on them.

"Now, I had hoped that would be the end of it," the inspector continued. "We picked up the boy's body, searched it, and buried it. He was just another terrorist, though they're beginning to send them awfully young. I continue a routine surveillance on Isaac and Rebecca, and they seem to be going about their business. The missionary goes home, and everybody gets a good night's rest.

"But then Isaac and Rebecca get together at four o'clock in the morning! And she leaves for Jerusalem, and I start getting that suspicious feeling again. How can I help it? What a cast of characters I have! What in the world are they up to?

"I have to order surveillance on Rebecca all the way down in Jerusalem. Is she going to talk to Arabs? Does she have some kind of report for somebody? Do the Palestinians want to know how their attack worked and is she going to give them the bad news? Why does she make that trip?"

Rebecca couldn't help but nearly sneer at this. How maddening to sit and listen to this arrogant policeman boast of his surveillance and his theories, tampering with one of the fine moments of her life! He seemed to be an intelligent and accommodating man, but his manner was repulsive.

The inspector must have read her mind. He looked straight at Rebecca and changed his tone entirely. Without a trace of the former sarcasm, he told her, "I'm sorry, young lady. I realize that you visited your father. And I respect him. I don't know if you are aware of what he actually does for Israel, but let me just say that I deeply respect Rabbi Bethuel. But you must let me do my work. I'm doing my part for Israel, too. If you are my enemy, I'll know that before you leave this room. Otherwise, well, I have already asked your forgiveness."

Immediately Rebecca felt sorry. This remarkable man was not within her power of judgment. She would keep silent until he questioned her, and then she would just tell him what had happened. She knew he would recognize the truth.

"Finally, my friends," the inspector went on, "and I feel satisfied that you really *are* my friends, I decided to get this meeting together and ask some simple questions. If you will each just answer me straightforwardly, I'm sure we can conclude these proceedings very soon. And I thank you in advance for cooperating."

The rest of the day was consumed in individual interviews with Inspector Cohen. Isaac was first, and he enlightened his interrogator with the news of his impending marriage to Rebecca.

"I'm delighted," the inspector said in sincerity. "Now I can see why she went to her father. At least it makes the trip *look* innocent," he continued, studying Isaac carefully.

Isaac had told him firmly, with all the assurance he could muster, that it was inconceivable that Rebecca was any sort of Palestinian agent, and that such suspicions of Israel's native-born citizens were obnoxious. "When will you have faith in your own people?" Isaac asked.

"When *Erezt Yisroel*, our homeland, is safe for Jews," the inspector told him. But Isaac was certain that when the inspector had finished with him, Rebecca was beyond suspicion.

Rebecca went in next to the little room adjoining the main area and simply related the events of the past three days. The inspector said nothing as she talked, watching her calmly and obviously evaluating her every word and gesture. "I believe you," he said simply when the interview concluded. "You and Isaac are free to go. We have already arranged a ride back for you."

The *mazkir* was not interrogated since this was just part of his work.

When the doctor entered the little room, the inspector rose and they embraced. They said simultaneously, "David," and "Joseph." The inspector apologized profusely to the doctor for the inconvenienced. Dr. ben Judah said simply, "I depend on your work. We all do."

The inspector's only question was about Joshua's character. The doctor told him, "He's a good man. I admire him very much." There were no questions about the doctor himself, whom the inspector knew well.

As Joshua was escorted into the interrogation room, a car drew up to the back door of the building to take the kibbutz members home. Isaac declined the ride, however, saying that he wanted to wait for Joshua to come back out.

Rebecca was as surprised as the agents. The redhead spoke up. "He's a friend of yours?"

"I feel responsible for his being involved," Isaac told him. The agents glanced at each other, but momentarily agreed that Isaac could do as he wished.

Rebecca immediately requested to stay also, asking Isaac's permission to wait with him.

He took her hand and thanked her. "Of course you can stay," he told her. The car left with the *mazkir* and Dr. ben Judah, the agents agreeing to provide a ride whenever the other two were ready. Finally Isaac and Rebecca were left alone in the courtroom.

Rebecca was glad for this opportunity, though she had wished it were under better circumstances. As they sat on a bench, hands enfolded, the bride-to-be explained to her groom the rabbi's preferences for their wedding. Isaac listened carefully to the remarkable traditions of his ancestors, all the while wondering how he could accomplish all the requirements.

In the interrogation room, the inspector was obviously a bit uncomfortable in Joshua's presence. "My questions for you," he began, "have to do with your loyalty to this nation. I don't meet a great many Hebrew Christians, and I don't know why you believe what you do. But let me tell you this, young man, if you're in any way involved with belittling this country, I'm going to see that you're deported. And if you helped those terrorists, you're going to spend the rest of your life in jail!"

"Any true follower of Jesus Christ loves Israel," Joshua answered quietly. "My Lord said that He came only to the lost sheep of the house of Israel."

"Was Jesus the Jewish Messiah?" Inspector Cohen asked suddenly.

Joshua looked carefully into the police officer's eyes, as if to detect whether his question were truly personal. Perhaps the inspector, like so many other Israelis, secretly wondered about the Jewish Carpenter who had preached His gospel exclusively in this land. Perhaps he, like Nicodemus before him, suspected that his own knowledge of things was insufficient to confront God. If his heart were spiritually hungry, he was talking to the right person. Joshua mentally asked God for immediate help with this lost soldier of Israel.

"Jesus was certainly the Jewish Messiah," Joshua answered. "And the Messiah of everyone else as well."

"Why did you go to help that terrorist?"

"He was a human being."

"He was a *Palestinian!*" the inspector thundered back, spitting out the term as though it were something unpleasant in his mouth. He glared at Joshua.

"He was a human being, dedicated to a cause. And he was dying. He never would have seen God if God had not sent me to him. If you were a Palestinian, you would probably be doing what he tried to do. And if you were dying, you would welcome anyone who would help—even from among your enemies. Why do you even ask me why I sent to see him?"

The inspector merely nodded, looking down at the surface of his desk and thinking. Finally he asked, "How many Jewish people believe in Jesus?"

"Not many," Joshua said, realizing that the inspector's suspicions about him had already been quieted. "But then, when we read our own Bible, we can see that only a remnant of our people were faithful to God at any time in the past. I often wonder if there are not just as many truly believing Jews—Jews who follow the Messiah—today as there ever were."

"I have read the New Testament," the inspector said quietly. "I find no fault with Jesus."

"Then why don't you come to Him? Why don't you believe in him?" Joshua asked with excitement in his voice. Was this Israeli actually going to confess Christ right here and now? Would he be saved, sitting in a police station?

"I could never become a Gentile. That's something I could never do. I could never be one of them. I would kill myself before I would do that," the inspector quietly assured the evangelist.

"But you don't become a Gentile when you believe in Jesus," Joshua told him, urging him to think deeply. "All of Jesus' followers were Jews. All His disciples and all the apostles came from our people. We founded the first church! We wrote the Bible! How could you possibly become a Gentile by following the Jewish Messiah?"

The inspector was silent, his face very grave. Doubtless what Joshua had said was affecting him. Whether it was news to the inspector that there is truth in the fact that following Christ is a Jewish act, or whether he had thought about it before, Joshua did not know. But he was thinking about it now that much was certain.

At last the inspector looked up at Joshua and began to slowly shake his head. "No," he said slowly. "No, it's not for me, despite what you say. I realize that the first Christians were Jews. But now the Gentiles have overtaken Christianity, and they have ruined it. I could follow Jesus, I suppose—there's nothing wrong with Jesus—but I could never be comfortable with Gentiles. I don't care how softly they speak or how earnestly they pray, Joshua. Gentiles kill Jews. They hate us, and they have always hated us. They came carrying crosses so many times in the past, and they killed our people and persecuted us. You yourself are fine, Joshua. I have no suspicion of you, and I respect you for what you did for that young boy. Do you think I'm not a human being, too? But I do not mix with Gentile people, and I have my reasons. I could never worship with them, no matter how much they protest that they love the Jews. I have yet to see them really love the Jews, and we have waited for that love for two thousand years, you know."

"You could worship with Jewish followers of Jesus right here in Israel," Joshua insisted. "You certainly don't have to become a Gentile to be a Christian."

"The interview is over, Joshua," the inspector said. "You may go."

Joshua didn't move. He only looked hopefully at the inspector. Was the a chance that his heart might be moved?

But the inspector rose from his chair, avoiding Joshua's eyes, and held the door open. The conversation was finished. Joshua, breathing thanks to the Lord for the seed he was able to sow, left the room.

As Joshua entered the courtroom, he was delighted to see Isaac still there, apparently waiting for him. Joshua approached him, and they shook hands warmly.

"I'm so glad you waited. Could we talk together?" he asked Isaac. He didn't seem at all wary of Isaac.

"That's what I want to do," Isaac told him. "Rebecca just went back to the kibbutz. She told me the most beautiful story about Israel in Jesus' time and there are some things I want to ask you. I suppose you know the New Testament and what was going in the first century here?"

"Well, a little. I'll try to help you if I can."

"Now, I don't want any help with Jesus, Joshua. Is that understood?" Isaac tried to sound very decisive and, in fact, he had little interest in Joshua's Messianic convictions. But, in truth, he was interested in the man; he was still impressed by Joshua, with his selfless devotion to the terrorist, his uncanny ability to sense and predict people's thoughts and his obvious strength of character. He assumed that the evangelist, as a man studied in the Bible, would have a great deal to say about Rebecca's father's information. And, frankly, he wanted some advice. Like many agnostics, he felt in his heart that a committed religious person had special insight. And he assumed that Joshua would not press the point about his Christianity, for he trusted that the Hebrew Christian would know when a case was hopeless.

But Joshua was thinking along completely different lines. He was thanking God for a secret blessing—something that he could sense was developing within Isaac. This would not be his first interview with a combative Jew who was in a tight spot. Obviously Isaac was not perfectly sure of what he should do with Rebecca and whatever it was that she had told him. He seemed uncomfortable emotionally and in need of help.

Thank you, Lord, Joshua prayed silently, *for bringing them around when the chips are down.*

As the two walked together out of the back door, Isaac told a security guard that he would find his own way back to the kibbutz. The man nodded. "I hope they don't follow us," Isaac said quietly to Joshua.

Joshua replied that he thought they wouldn't "In any case, I know a nice hillside that overlooks the sea," he said, "if you're up to walking about three miles. I don't think they've bugged it yet."

As they walked along through pleasant

Tiberias, Isaac filled Joshua in on the events that had transpired since they last talked. Joshua was a little surprised but very pleased that Isaac had already proposed to Rebecca. "You've done the right thing," he assured Isaac. Isaac tried to apologize for the problem with the police, but Joshua told him that he understood completely and appreciated their care about what had transpired at the kibbutz. They both agreed that Israel was not a peaceful place to live. "Not yet, anyway," Joshua said.

When they had arrived at the lovely spot Joshua knew about, they sat on a grassy knoll and looked over the magnificent Sea of Galilee below. It was nearly evening and the water shimmered in the setting sun.

"If you'll spare me your evangelism," Isaac began, "I want to ask your advice about my wedding plans. With all your faults"—Isaac smiled as he said this—"you seem like a very smart man."

"I'm honored," Joshua said. "What's the problem?"

NINE

Rebecca, back in her quarters at the kibbutz, was glad to have a moment to herself. Without a doubt, the past few days had been the strangest and most exciting of her life.

She had aimed her machine gun at the door of the kibbutz nursery, fully expecting a frontal assault by the Palestinians; she had witnessed the peaceful death of an enemy of the state; she had heard the doctrine of a Christian evangelist; she had been courted and proposed to by the man she somehow knew was God's man for her; she had visited her father in Jerusalem; she had been followed and apprehended by the police, and interrogated as if she were a terrorist sympathizer; and she had explained, in a few short moments she'd had with her fiancé, her father's preferences for their wedding.

She decided that she had earned a good rest. She actually hoped Isaac would not call on her that evening. She thought she would wash her hair and bathe and simply go to bed early, but then her father's admonitions came to mind— the bride was to be waiting every night. She resolved to do her personal ministrations but also to wait up for Isaac. It was his privilege to call on her any night, as she understood things now, and even to carry her off to his bridal chamber. Her head full of romance, she laid a flashlight near the door, testing it first to be sure the batteries were working. This would be her lamp, she thought, filled with oil. If the bridegroom came tonight, she would be ready.

She smiled to herself as she bathed, remembering Isaac's almost comic reaction to her father's wedding custom story. The young man had been astounded; he had whispered in the courtroom, "Rebecca, this is the twentieth century! How can we do all that? My father is eight thousand miles from here! And I don't have any money to give your father!" At that, Rebecca had pouted and asked, "Do you expect to get me for nothing?" As he had started to protest, she had kissed him quickly on the mouth to show that she had only been teasing. It also served to show Isaac that he need not take her father's wishes so literally. She was just going to leave it up to him to find a compromise.

Isaac had understood that he was to find some approximation of the ancient customs to please her father. Perhaps a nice hotel room overlooking the sea could be the bridal chamber, and maybe he could give her father some token for the price. As for the other requirements, they could easily drink a cup of wine together, and he would gladly sign any sort of contract that would get him Rebecca. He was certainly not in favor of the waiting period, so he would have to find a way out of that.

Rebecca knew that Isaac realized that the spirit of the wedding customs was what the rabbi wished to see maintained; he wanted to be honored for having raised a daughter in the best of Jewish tradition. Well, why not?

Rebecca had been proud of Isaac when he announced that he wanted to wait for Joshua. She had noticed how alone Joshua had been at the hearing, and how he automatically came under suspicion. He was the strange one, by the reckoning of the police, but Rebecca still liked the man. His religion aside, Joshua was a rare man. She approved of Isaac for appreciating him. And she also knew that Isaac needed to talk to another man at this point. He was a loner around the kibbutz, she had sense; he had not spoken of having close friends here. Perhaps his American accent had put the young Israelis off. Joshua, an outsider to the kibbutz but a man who knew Rebecca, however slightly, might serve as a friend for the moment.

Rebecca was humming quietly in amusement as she thought of Isaac and Joshua sitting somewhere alone in Tiberias, with Isaac asking, "Should I marry her immediately? Do you think I should wait? What about those things her father told her?" Rebecca was not at all concerned about Isaac choosing to wait a while before the wedding. Her intuition about Isaac told her that the man had never been in love before, and now he was going to seize his opportunity. He would find a way to satisfy her father and still become her husband in the shortest possible time. And she was deeply satisfied by that idea.

Rebecca's intuitions were accurate. Isaac was at that moment asking Joshua similar questions as they sat together on the hillside watching the sea. He *did* need a friend, and a friend outside the kibbutz circles. He wanted information about the Israeli wedding customs of the first century, for one thing, and oddly, it was not available among the modern Israeli natives. Only a New Testament scholar seemed adequate to evaluate the traditions explained by Rebecca's father, the modern Israelis of Isaac's acquaintance being so much more concerned with building an up-to-date secular nation.

And in his heart he knew that Joshua was wise. The evangelist, who had first sensed the love between Isaac and Rebecca, could give good counsel, and Isaac knew it. He was eager to unburden his heart, to catch his breath, and to share with someone trustworthy all his thoughts of the past few days. He felt inexplicably drawn to the strong character of the missionary.

Isaac had begun by telling Joshua the wedding custom in all its detail as he had heard it from Rebecca in the courtroom. Joshua was silent as Isaac explained the covenant, the cup, the price, the bridegroom leaving to build the chamber, the bride waiting in consecration, the "abduction" in the night, and the marriage supper. As he reviewed the various steps of the procedure, Joshua was looking out at the sea, the smallest smile turning his lips upward and his eyes absolutely glowing. Isaac thought to himself that Joshua was indeed proud of his ancestry, regardless of his religious beliefs.

When Isaac had finished, Joshua said fervently, "Praise God!"

"It's a beautiful tradition, I must admit," Isaac said, "but what am I going to do with it? Do you think Rebecca really wants me to fulfill all that? How can I do it?"

"Praise God!" Joshua said again, and he shook his head back and forth in some secret joy.

"All right, praise God," Isaac echoed. "It's a lovely story. But is it accurate, is it worth while, and did our people actually do those things? Help me out, please!"

Isaac was a bit impatient, Joshua saw, and a bit uncomfortable. The missionary was in possession of great knowledge where this wedding tradition was concerned, but how was he going to persuade Isaac to hear him out? Joshua had the secret knowledge that God's Spirit was working in Isaac's life and that this was the young man's real reason for consulting him. Joshua perceived that their interview had been arranged by God Himself; Isaac was being called to faith in the Messiah.

"To begin with," Joshua said calmly, "I'm going to have to talk about Jesus, no matter what you think about Him. This particular first-century tradition can't be explained without reference to Jesus. If you want an explanation, I have it, but it concerns the Messiah, and that's all there is to that. If you like, I'll tie you to a tree and you can tell your friends you were forced to listen to the gospel!"

Isaac only smiled and shook his head. "You just never give up, do you?" he said. "Joshua, you can talk about whatever you want, but please understand, if your motive is to make a Christian out of me, you're wasting your time. And you wouldn't be doing me any good service either, I can tell you."

"All right," countered Joshua, "I'm not going to sit here and tell you the whole New Testament. I only want to talk about Jesus as a Bridegroom. That's what you are, after all."

Isaac was amazed. "Jesus as a Bridegroom? Are you kidding? Did *He* get married?"

"Well, not as yet, But we might say He's engaged."

Now Isaac was curious. What sort of strange philosophy was this? Jesus Christ engaged to be married? That was a new one on him. He looked at Joshua skeptically. "Go ahead," he said, "I'll listen."

"Do you mind if I quote from an ancient Jewish book?" Joshua asked him.

"Not at all," Isaac said, and then saw Joshua taking a tattered copy of the New Testament out of his shirt pocket. It was one of the miniature

137

Bibles that were the stock in trade of the street missionary, Isaac knew, and for a moment he wanted to object. But his curiosity overcame his aversions, so he said nothing. He did favor Joshua with a supercilious smile that said, "OK, one point for you."

Joshua looked at Isaac, eye to eye, with a serious expression. "I want you to listen closely, dear brother. I think this is very important information for you to have. I realize you're not very fond of this Book, but remember, it was you who came to me with the question about the Jewish marriage tradition. The answers to all of your questions are in this Book."

Isaac nodded, determined to hear Joshua out. He felt a slight stirring in his heart that was somehow related to his gratitude that Joshua would take the time to teach him, even though it was not his favorite kind of lesson. He could feel that the missionary cared about him.

"I want to discuss your marriage tradition step by step, and I'll begin in the book of Hebrews," Joshua told him. "This book is a letter written to the Jews, of course, and what it says is of concern to every Jew."

"Go on," Isaac said with a sigh. "Do your worst!"

As Joshua opened his Bible, Isaac sensed that the missionary had a heartfelt reverence for it. He opened the pocket-size Book carefully, leafing through the pages slowly, so as not to damage them. Isaac could not help but think of the old men in the synagogue of his youth who kissed the facing pages of the Scriptures, and who virtually caressed their prayer books as they read.

"The author writes," Joshua began, "about the old covenant and the new covenant in Chapter 8 of Hebrews. He compares the system of the ancient priesthood with the new covenant brought by Jesus to the Jews. He says in verses 8 and 9, 'Behold, the days come, saith the Lord, when I will make a new covenant with the house of Israel and with the house of Judah: not according to the covenant that I made with their fathers in the day when I took them by the hand to lead them out of the land of Egypt.' God actually was replacing the old system of laws with a new system."

"Well, you can find whatever you want in the New Testament, I suppose," Isaac objected.

"But the writer is quoting Jeremiah here. The words I just gave you also appear in Jeremiah 31:31–32. Our own prophet had announced this new covenant."

"There's a *new* covenant in the *Old* Testament?" Isaac asked a bit skeptically.

"Yes, of course, and it has to do with the Messiah's coming. The new covenant had to be signed in blood. Remember, Abraham had to divide animals when he received the covenant from God that made us chosen people. And Moses had to sacrifice, too. It's the blood that makes the covenant go into effect."

"Go on," Isaac said, hoping he wasn't going to hear a lot about the "shed blood of Christ," that missionary catch phrase that always bothered him somehow.

"Well, it's very simple. The Messiah came like a sacrificial animal and gave His blood to seal the new covenant. John the Baptist called Him 'the Lamb of God, which taketh away the sin of the world.'* Isaiah said the Messiah would come as a lamb to the slaughter." Joshua was looking at him with open, honest eyes, as if to to ask, "What could be simpler?"

Isaac told him, "This is sounding awfully Christian."

"I'm quoting only Jews," Joshua retorted, truthfully enough.

"How does this new covenant become a wedding contract?" Isaac asked.

"Well, the relationship of God and Israel has always been a marriage. The book of Hosea spells that out clearly. And Jeremiah's language in announcing the new covenant is very interesting; he says, 'My covenant they brake, although I was an *husband* unto them.'† God was a disappointed Bridegroom when we failed to keep the old laws. But Paul, another Jew of course, explained marriage by saying, 'This is a great mystery: but I speak concerning Christ and the church.'‡ The proper relationship be-

*John 1:29
†Jeremiah 31:32b
‡Ephesians 5:32

tween the believers and the Messiah could constitute a happy marriage for God. The church is called the Bride of Christ."

"Why are there so few Jews in this Church, Joshua? Aren't we the ones supposed to be getting married?" Although Isaac was feeling a bit uncomfortable, he realized that Joshua's Bible quoting was accurate.

"I don't know about you," Joshua said softly, "but I'm certainly going to that wedding with the Lord. The Gentiles in the church haven't always cared for our people as they were supposed to, but the Messiah said, 'I was sent only to the lost sheep of the house of Israel.'§ Believe me, He rejoices when one of His own signs that wedding contract."

"How can all those Gentiles get into a covenant made with Israel anyway? That seems a little strange."

"Paul says Gentiles become grafted into the Jewish tree when by faith they come to the Jewish Messiah. They become chosen like us. They're called the spiritual seed of Abraham."

"I like Jews better," Isaac carped.

"So come to the Kingdom with me. There will be plenty of Jews there. You'd be surprised to know what goes on in a lot of Jewish hearts."

"All right," Isaac said patiently, "suppose I accept that this new covenant is a wedding contract. Where's the rest of the Jewish wedding?

§Matthew 15:23, NASB

141

What about our cup and the price and the bridal chamber? Surely your Messiah didn't do all that."

"You underestimate our Messiah," Joshua told him. "He did it all, and so beautifully. He drank the cup at the Passover table, and He said, 'This is my blood of the new testament, which is shed for many for the remission of sins.'[1] In the new covenant, God promises, 'I will forgive their iniquity, and I will remember their sins no more.'[**] Jesus put that into effect when He drank the cup. He redeemed us. you know very well what that cup is called—the cup we drink with the hidden piece of bread."

"The Cup of Redemption," Isaac found himself whispering, remembering back to his father's Passover table. He felt chills as he said it.

Truly, Joshua seemed very persuasive and certain of his beliefs, Isaac thought. But that was only to be expected. If the man had committed his life to being a missionary to the Jews, he would certainly be good at it and know the right things to say. He would be ready in every way to reach into the Jewish heart and soul. This was his profession, after all.

And yet there was something more to Joshua, Isaac had to admit. The man was kind, loving, almost tender. He never became impatient. He couldn't be insulted, not even about his faith. Every minute he had spent with the missionary,

[1]Matthew 26:28
[**]Jeremiah 31:34

142

Isaac had seen Joshua in uncomplaining service to others. How like his idea of his Lord Joshua really was. He could apply the Scriptures as well as a rabbi, maybe even more skillfully. But the most noticeable thing about him was his love; it reached out.

The case he was presently making about the wedding custom was convincing so far, and Isaac didn't doubt that Joshua would teach him a great deal. But more convincing still was the man himself. Somehow Isaac felt good just sitting next to him. Whatever it was that made Joshua the man he was, Isaac realized that he wanted it. Short of completely changing his religion, Isaac suddenly knew he would follow Joshua anywhere.

Joshua was unlike the rabbis Isaac had known in his youth. They had been remote, busy men, carrying themselves with the bearing of deeply learned scholars. Some were sensitive, kind men, it could be easily seen; but others were hypocrites, Isaac knew. An assistant rabbi in the large synagogue of his youth had affected a European dialect, although he had been born and educated in New York, because he felt it added to his credibility as a spiritual leader to appear to be foreign, a scholar from the ghetto. Isaac never liked phony things; he had given his life to Israel in order to be real. Joshua was real, and there was no taking that away from him. Isaac would have preferred that Joshua were a rabbi rather than a Christian missionary, but the man was genuine, and worth hearing out.

"Tell me about the price," Isaac said, turning from his thoughts to the silent Joshua as he became conscious of that fact that Joshua had waited out his thought process. He conceded, "I can accept your explanation of the cup. But did Jesus pay the price for His Bride?"

"You know the answer to that, don't you?" Joshua answered.

"Are you talking about the crucifixion?"

"I wouldn't have wanted to pay that high a price," Joshua said quietly, and Isaac could almost see the very pain of Jesus reflected on Joshua's face. "You know, in the Garden of Gethsemane He prayed, 'Father, if thou be willing, remove this cup from me: nevertheless not my will, but thine, be done.'[††] And His sweat fell like great drops of blood while He was contemplating the cross. The crucifixion was the highest price any bridegroom ever paid, I'm sure."

"He didn't *want* to be crucified?" Isaac asked.

"Would you?" Joshua answered. "No, actually He didn't want to be crucified. He was in human flesh, for our sakes, and human flesh suffers in crucifixion. But the force of that passage is that He was obedient to His Father's will. I imagine some Jewish bridegrooms came back to their fathers after learning the bride price and asked their fathers' advice about whether it was worth it. The smart one must have said, 'Your will, not

[††]Luke 22:42

144

mine, be done.' They accepted their fathers' desires."

"What did Jesus' Father say?"

"He sent an angel to strengthen His Son, the Scripture says. That was His answer. Jesus paid the price for us,"

"And then He left His Bride?"

"Right. He went back to His Father in heaven after His resurrection. He had even made the typical bridegroom's speech: 'I go to prepare a place for you.'[‡‡] And He went, like any Jewish bridegroom, back to His Father's house."

It was compelling, Isaac had to admit. Remarkably, Jesus seemed to have fulfilled this Jewish wedding tradition, at least as far as they had gone with it. And very exactly, not just in symbol. Isaac did not doubt the scholarship of Rebecca's father; she had filled him in on the man's vast knowledge of Jewish custom. But how had he come up with such a Christian doctrine? Were Judaism and Christianity really that much alike? Had Jesus performed a vast Jewish courtship in calling out His followers? Isaac had to know more.

"What's next? That's all that's happened, isn't it? Rebecca's father said the groom was to return for the bride, by surprise. Jesus has never returned. Has something gone wrong?"

"No, I don't think so. I think He's still at His Father's house preparing our place. And we're waiting for Him to return. We're waiting in a

‡‡John 14:2b

145

consecrated way—set apart, bought with a price. We are to act like the covenanted Bride, and be waiting at all times for our Bridegroom to come. We are to have oil in our lamps and be ready to travel, even at night. Our oil is the Holy Spirit, the third Person in the Trinity, who came to the Jews at Pentecost after the Messiah ascended. We are each filled with the Holy Spirit and ready to go at any moment."

"All right," said Isaac, actually holding up his hand as if to stop the inpouring of the effective Bible study Joshua was teaching. "It's a very beautiful story, but it's not enough for you to say that He's coming back. Every Christian has been believing that doctrine for two thousand years, and millions of people have lived and died in hopelessness. Nothing has happened. What assurance do you have that anything will ever happen?"

"Do you trust prophecy?" Joshua asked him.

"Well—" Isaac felt trapped. How could he say he didn't trust the Jewish prophets? Yet he was sure that Joshua was going to prove his case with prophecy, and he wanted to scream out, "Don't go any further, I can't stand it!" He felt his whole mind swaying toward Joshua's logic and his impelling spiritual grasp. The story seemed true, and if true, very important. He finally managed to say weakly, "There are many interpretations of prophecy."

"Do you believe the prophecies about our people returning to this land and rebuilding it?

Do you believe the desert can blossom like a rose? Do you believe that God can regather the Jewish people?"

Isaac's reply made him feel ashamed of himself. He found himself saying defensively, "it could be a coincidence."

Joshua could feel Isaac's pain. But he pressed on with more prophecy, and more devastating argument. "Have you seen the town of Ashkelon on the Mediterranean coast? Do you realize that immigrants are living there now in the old houses of the Philistines? Do you believe Zephaniah 2:7: 'And the coast shall be for the remnant of the house of Judah; they shall feed thereupon: in the houses of Ashkelon shall they lie down in the evening: for the Lord their God shall visit them, and turn away their captivity' "?

Isaac knew the truth of it, and he knew something else, too. He knew he wanted to cry, or to throw himself into the arms of this incredible Joshua, whose every word cut right to his heart. He kept his thoughts to himself, though, mastering his emotions with difficulty. He was quiet for a long moment before finding his voice. Then, as calmly as he could, he said, "What does prophecy say about the return of the Messiah for His Bride?"

Joshua fully appreciated Isaac's courage and resolve. He had been in this position before. Isaac, he could see, was beginning to find the Lord in his heart, and the Scriptures were doing their promised task. The Word of God would never return void.

Joshua's ministry was always like this. While the Jewish people rejected him out of hand, while they fought the gospel with everything they had, they still possessed an inner respect for the truth. They would never defame the prophets and they would never think that the Bible lies. A little light always went a long way with the Jewish people. Joshua had witnessed to many a Gentile atheist in his time, and the going actually had been tougher. It was never necessary to argue God's existence with any Jew no matter how antagonistic that Jew might be toward the gospel. When the conversation grew intimate, the Jew invariably relented. He had to. That was how God made him.

Whether this miracle—Isaac coming to him with the gospel virtually coming out of his own mouth in the form of this ancient Jewish wedding custom—would bring this Jew to the Lord was unclear. But it was certain that he would gain a new appreciation for the Lord and for the truth. He would never be quite the same again.

And perhaps, there by the very sea upon which the Lord had once walked, the man would give his heart fully to God. Perhaps the time was right for him to receive Christ as his Saviour. God seemed to have taken quite a hand in the affairs of Isaac—bringing Rebecca and Joshua into his life at the same time, making Isaac think about death through the death of the terrorist, causing Isaac to watch as that dying boy came to real faith. God wanted Isaac, Joshua knew.

With a prayer humming in the back of his mind, Joshua prepared to explain the most subtle part of Isaac's wedding tradition, the part played by prophecy. To show Isaac the Scriptures that had already come to pass was one thing; demonstrating the future was quite another. Would he be able to see that the Bible contains an accurate history of the future? Would he appreciate that all that had been prophesied would surely come to pass, as surely as Israel was theirs and the Jews occupied Ashkelon? Or would he scoff and call it all Christian dreaming?

"Let me answer you concerning the prophecy about this wedding custom," Joshua began. "And let me assure you that the prophets saw it all. The Lord will return for His Bride, there will be a bridal chamber in heaven, where Jesus and the church will spend seven years—like the ancient seven days—and there will be a marriage supper like the Jews used to have. Every detail of Jesus' great wedding will be accomplished, and it will be carried out in the exact traditions of the Jewish people."

Isaac sat perfectly silent, looking at the sea.

"Because," continued Joshua, *"Jesus is Jewish!"*

TEN

"He might return before we finish talking," Joshua stated dramatically. "He might come to take me to His Father's house while you sit here."

"And He won't take me?" Isaac asked, a bit cynically.

"You haven't responded to His proposal," Joshua said. "The Messiah said His own sheep would hear His voice. You know very well, when the trumpet sounds the harvest is over. There has to be a cut-off point somewhere. The bride who is ready goes to the wedding when the bridegroom comes."

"Well, what's your prophetic proof of all that? It just sounds like so much church doctrine to me."

"Think about our holy days for a moment. *Shuvuot*—Pentecost—that's the harvest holiday. All summer following Pentecost the people plant and till the ground. But when the trumpet sounds, on what we now call *Rosh Hashanah*, the old Feast of Trumpets, the crops are in and the harvest is finished. Jeremiah, just to mention one prophet, could see that we wouldn't be ready—not all of us. "The summer is ended, now we are not saved,'* he said. The Bible says, 'Now is the accepted time' "† Joshua concluded, with a pointed look at Isaac.

Isaac was silent, wrestling with an inner conflict. Somewhere, somehow, deep in his heart he felt the logic of all this. He was no Bible reader, but he knew that God had to act again someday on behalf of the Jewish people. Surely those long-ago promises would be honored in Israel; surely the Father meant to bring His most glorious plans to fruition. In the manner that the Jews expected a Messiah, Isaac had expected some act of God all his life. Whether or not Joshua was rendering the Scriptures fairly, Isaac felt a rightness about it.

"Now, Paul gave us a wonderful picture of that moment when the groom will return for His bride," Joshua went on. " 'For the Lord himself shall descend from heaven with a shout, with the voice of the archangel, and with the trump of God: and the dead in Christ shall rise first: then we which are alive and remain shall be caught up together with them in the clouds, to meet the Lord in the air: and so shall we ever be with the Lord.'‡ That fulfills everything. You have the shout of the bridegroom to notify the bride of his coming; you have the trumpet to finish the harvest and to proclaim liberty for God's people.

*Jeremiah 8:20
†2 Corinthians 6:2
‡1 Thessalonians 4:16–17

We used to blow that trumpet on each Jubilee to proclaim liberty, you remember.[§] Well, this is *real* liberty!"

Isaac just shook his head in skepticism. "Now, just wait a minute. It's all very beautiful, very lovely, very fitting. But you suddenly are throwing in some obscure vision of Paul from the New Testament, and it seems disconnected from everything else. So what if a few symbols come up? Who knows what they really mean—shouts, trumpets? Certainly we can't live our lives sensibly on the basis of such mythology. Where did Paul get such a crazy idea—meeting the Lord in the clouds! What's the Old Testament basis for that?"

"Easy," said Joshua confidently. "This won't be the first time God used shouts and trumpets to take His people to their 'Promised Land.' Do you remember how we got through the walls of Jericho to begin with, the first time our people came to Israel?"

Isaac was struck. Of course he knew the biblical story of how Joshua had entered the land with the shouts of the people and the trumpet blasts which felled the walls of Jericho.[¶] He couldn't help glancing at Joshua with appreciation of this singularly clear symbol.

Joshua went on, "And what's the Israeli name for Jesus? Isn't He also *Yeshua*—Joshua? Isn't this a repeat performance? You want an Old Testament basis for this miracle—I wish you

§Leviticus 25:10
¶Joshua 6:5

152

had been with Joshua! You would have seen so clearly how powerful God is when He brings His people home!

Could it be true? Isaac found himself thinking. *How remarkable! How coincidental, at least. An anointed One coming again to Israel—to the whole world, in fact—to take the believers to the promised land. Could it be true?*

In all good faith, Isaac wanted to believe that. If only all the pointlessness of life had some point; if only God were really to make Himself known again in the world. And truly, the way Joshua was putting it, it all seemed very believable. How like the Jewish wedding the coming of the Messiah would be, according to what Joshua was explaining. How well the New Testament coordinated with the Old. Was it an accident, a coincidence? Was this man believing fables and forcing Scripture to conform? Was Joshua deluded? Somehow Isaac couldn't accept that Joshua was deluded. This Joshua, like the Joshua of the Jericho campaign, and yes, like the Joshua from Nazareth, was a speaker of the truth. It would be hard to fault this missionary. His character and his veracity seemed unquestionable.

In the deepest part of his own heart Isaac knew he was hungry. He had always wanted there to be a personal God, a God he could reach and a God he could relate to. Surely God was not the distant, judgmental, fearsome figure he had been taught to revere in his youth. Not if He was the Painter of the wild flowers and the Design-er of the movements of the planets. How could that be? Surely God was compassionate, caring, loving. Surely He was just and merciful. Sure-ly He was like Joshua's concept of the Messiah. Perhaps God was like Jesus—or Jesus like God. Perhaps indeed the gentle Preacher from Galilee represented God. Perhaps God was like that.

"Shall I go on?" Joshua interrupted. Isaac realized that Joshua had been watching him carefully as his thoughts progressed. "There's more to say about your wedding procedure," Joshua told him gently. Isaac just nodded, not quite trusting his voice. If Joshua knew what Isaac was thinking, he might start insisting that Isaac be "saved" on the spot.

Joshua *did* know pretty well what Isaac was thinking, since he was an experienced testifier for the Lord and a missionary of prayerful sen-sitivity. He could see that Isaac had been moved by the portion of the message he had heard so far, and that his heart was opening like a flower. But he would not pounce on Isaac, as if he were the opponent in a debate. People came to the Lord ever so slowly, ever so gently—particular-ly Jewish people. Joshua could sense that Isaac was ready, but his moment of salvation was up to Isaac and the Lord. Joshua would merely continue to teach to the Word of God.

"And so just as the bridegroom calls for his bride rather suddenly, and takes her off to his father's house," he continued, "Jesus will take away the believers quickly—'in the twinkling of an eye.'** the Scripture says. The Bride is to be ready and waiting. She will have her veil on, of course, and so the people who may see her pass through the streets will not know who she is. The people of the world today certainly don't recognize the Bride of Christ. They see churches and people going into them, but they don't appreciate the Bride as a bride. It's as though the true believers are wearing a kind of spiritual veil and are not recognizable to the unbelievers. Even when this great wedding takes place, the rest of the world will go on as it was, after the Bride has departed in her veil."

Joshua paused, but Isaac was silent, slowly nodding.

"In the old days the wedding party would go through the streets by the light of their oil lamps. The bride had to have her lamp trimmed and ready, of course—you mentioned that. Well, the oil is the Holy Spirit. Believers are indwelt by the Holy Spirit. Oil is what God used to anoint His saints and He still uses it in the form of the Spirit. The Old Testament symbol is the Menorah, the candelabrum in the tabernacle; it was lit just once, but the priests replenished the oil constantly. So the believer in the Messiah receives the light of the world once, but he is constantly indwelt by the Spirit. In this way his light shines on others; anyone close to him can see it clearly. And you know, a flame is a beautiful symbol of

**1 Corinthians 15:52

155

the faith in the Messiah; a flame can ignite one hundred other flames without being diminished itself. And Jesus is called the light of the world."

Isaac was again quiet when Joshua paused. He was concentrating, Joshua could see. The missionary continued the lesson.

"When the bride and groom finally arrived at the groom's father's house, they would find quite an assembly of wedding guests—friends of the groom's father. Well, so will the believers when the Messiah brings them to heaven, His Father's house. The friends of His Father are the Old Testament saints. Abraham, Isaac, and Jacob will attend this wedding, along with the prophets and the faithful chosen people of the centuries before the coming of the Messiah. We will get quite a reception, I expect.

"But the celebration won't begin when we arrive. As you pointed out in your story of the wedding custom, the bride and groom must first go into the chamber for the seven days. And the groom's friend will wait outside until he hears the groom's voice. He will tell the guests when the wedding is consummated."

"That sounds like a rather unsavory ancient practice," Isaac broke in. "What's the New Testament equivalent of that?"

"Let me read John 3:29 for you," Joshua said, getting out his little Bible again. "The practice may seem unsavory to the natural mind," Joshua

156

said, as he leafed through the pages, "but it's an important little symbol in this wedding."

Joshua found the Scripture and said, "Now listen carefully, and understand. The Pharisees had been asking John the Baptist if he were the Messiah. In a way, they would have preferred him to say he was. They could put up with a 'Messiah' who stayed out in the desert and preached repentance to a few ascetics. The One they could not abide was the gentile Carpenter of Galilee, with whom none of them could argue. But John set them straight: 'He that hath the bride is the bridegroom: but the friend of the bridegroom, which standeth and heareth him, rejoiceth greatly because of the bridegroom's voice: this my joy therefore is fulfilled.' "

"Beautiful," Isaac said helplessly.

"When the bridegroom's voice is heard, the marriage is accomplished," Joshua pressed on. "A Scripture like that one is much more clear to Jews who knew their heritage than to Gentiles. Praise God that He gave you such knowledge!"

"Joshua, why do you say, 'Praise God'? Rebecca's father gave me this knowledge, and he certainly wasn't trying to lead me to Jesus Christ!"

"Isaac, anyone who tells the truth about Judaism leads you to Jesus Christ. And I praise God for this knowledge, because it was God who called out our people and gave them this glorious Messiah. Believe me, when any man speaks the truth, he is talking in some way about God and God has led him to speak. 'Every one that is of the truth heareth my voice,'†† the Messiah said."

Isaac was silent, and Joshua duly noted the lesser strength of his objections. Isaac was being "convicted," as the Christian usually put it, about the truth of the gospel. Joshua went on with his explanations.

"Now, you might wonder about the idea of a 'honeymoon' in heaven, but there is one. The Scriptures call it the judgment seat of Christ. We will all go before the Messiah in heaven and He will look at our works done for Him in the flesh. All of us on earth who believe in Him are His servants, and we do both good works and bad. Paul wrote to the Corinthians, in 1 Corinthians 3:11–15, that men's works will be graded. Some works are as valuable as gold, silver, and precious stones, and some only amount to wood, hay, and stubble. The Lord will use fire on these works, and we'll all see what burns up."

"Now, that's the trouble with your Christianity," Isaac broke in. "Judgment. I commit a little sin, and God will punish me. That's not how I picture things."

"Who said anything about sin?" Joshua countered. "God isn't punishing us for sins. All of man's sins were taken care of at the cross. Jesus is not going to charge you for what is already paid for. I was talking about *works*, not sins. The Messiah never punished a sinner."

"Everybody's sins are forgiven?"

†† John 18:37

"Yes, if they'll just accept the forgiveness."

"I don't feel forgiven," Isaac said heavily. "I never have."

"I do," Joshua said simply.

There was a pause as Isaac reflected. "Will He forgive me?"

"Certainly," Joshua assured him. "He surely didn't go to all the trouble of paying for your sins to refuse you! Look, He's providing a 'gift certificate.' When somebody gives you a gift certificate, you just take it to the store and claim the gift. You don't have to pay anything; the giver has already paid. That's the message of the gospel in the simplest terms."

Isaac's face was aglow with the possibilities, but he wanted to hear still more. He came back to the wedding custom, "How is this judgment seat like a honeymoon? It sounds like official business to me."

"Well, a honeymoon is where the groom removes the bride's veil and knows her secrets. Some honeymoons are disasters, let's face it, but love is the healing factor. Whatever happens up there, we'll be with the Messiah who loves us. Believe me, nobody's going to fall back out of heaven. When Peter pulled up his heavy fishing net, after the Lord directed him where to fish, the net didn't break and no fish fell out. And the disciples became fishers of men, just as the Lord promised. You're perfectly safe and your salvation is guaranteed once you believe in the Messiah. If you want to look forward to a good

159

honeymoon, then follow the Lord and do your good works for Him. But in any case, just know that He went to quite a lot of trouble to get you there, and He's going to be very glad to see you."

"What happens next?" Isaac asked, referring to the wedding again.

"All right, the announcement is made that the marriage is consummated—the saints have their crowns, and the Lord has examined them all. And then the celebrating begins outside the chamber. The marriage is now official, and the guests can rejoice. All of the celebrating will culminate in heaven in a great marriage supper— what we could call the reception and the Bride will be greatly honored. Revelation 19:7–8 says: 'Let us be glad and rejoice, and give honour to him: for the marriage of the Lamb is come, and his wife hath made herself ready. And to her was granted that she should be arrayed in fine linen, clean and white: for the fine linen is the righteousness of saints.' Notice how the Scripture now says 'wife' instead of 'bride.' The honeymoon is finished and we are now married to the Lord. How accurate God's word is! And then after the super we'll leave to live in our Bridegroom's Kingdom. We'll leave His Father's house and claim our sweetest time on earth, and we'll reign with our Husband in the Kingdom of God for a thousand years!"

"Joshua, it sounds wonderful," Isaac said in a small, hopeful voice. "It sounds wonderful." He did not speak further, not trusting his voice at this point. It was obvious to him that Joshua could see his spiritual hunger getting the better of his resistance.

As Joshua pictured the glorious marriage supper further, he said, "What a moment to look forward to, Isaac! Think of it! There we are, arrayed in white linen, the queen of the Kingdom! Perfected saints! All our sins paid for, all our good works rewarded. The Scriptures say that we will give our crowns to the Lord as a wedding gift! How fitting! Isaac, even John, as an old man, looked forward to being a bride. How he longed for the Lord's coming! The Romans left him on a barren island, Patmos, a stone quarry where practically nothing grew. He was supposed to slowly starve to death, but he saw the revelation of Jesus Christ instead! And He said, at the end of the wonderful revelation, 'Amen. Even so, come, Lord Jesus!'[††] He was so eager to see the Messiah come!"

"Joshua," Isaac began slowly. "I'm eager to see Him come, too. If He's really coming, I want to see that. Any man would want to see that. But if John was waiting for Him on that island nineteen hundred years ago and He didn't come, what makes you think He'll come now? Isn't the whole thing a little disappointing?"

"Not to me, Isaac. I believe in Him and I know He's coming. It wasn't up to the bride to pick the wedding day, you remember. The bridegroom's father, the host of the whole wedding, picked the

[††]Revelation 22:20

day. 'Only my Father knows.'§§ Jesus said. But it *was* up to the bride to be waiting. She waited every day, no matter how long it took. I have a wedding contract, a covenant with Jesus Christ. I've never grown tired of waiting for Him! If He doesn't come now, He'll come for me after I 'fall asleep.' But either way He'll come for me. And I'll be ready!"

"Has He come for the terrorist at the kibbutz?" Isaac asked suddenly.

"You loved him, didn't you?" Joshua asked.

Isaac thought a moment. "Yes, I loved him," he said quietly. "I wanted him to live."

"You have your wish," Joshua told him. "He's alive. He's with the Lord. He'll be at the wedding."

There was a long silence then as Isaac digested all he had heard. Joshua did not intrude on his private thoughts.

Isaac was looking out at the Sea of Galilee, realizing that they were not far from the site of Jesus' Sermon on the Mount. He could see the wild flowers the Galilean referred to when He said, "Consider the lilies of the field."¶¶ He could see the fishing boats on the sea. He could almost see the hurrying group of disciples, those common fishermen and tax collectors who followed their Messiah over these same hills and dales,

§§See Matthew 24:36
¶¶Matthew 6:28

learning the will of God, as He taught it. It was simply overwhelming.

Isaac spoke very slowly and distinctly. "Joshua, is it really true?"

Joshua said quietly, "It really is. All of it. He is our Messiah."

Isaac continued to look at the sea. "This is very important to me, Joshua," he said at length. "I must know if it is true."

"I didn't make up the wedding custom, Isaac. You brought it to me, from a Jew. And I didn't make up the Scriptures. The Bible is a Jew- ish book, an Israeli Book. Our ancestors were right, the prophets were right. They saw the Messiah coming, and He came. 'Salvation is of the Jews,'*** the Messiah said."

"Then why did they kill Him?" Isaac asked, with some bitterness.

"*I* killed Him, Isaac. Because of me—because of the extent of my crimes—He had to go to the cross. It was the only way a just God could for- give me. I killed Him with my sins. And you killed Him, too. Those who put Him on the cross didn't know what they were really doing. He said from the cross, 'Father, forgive them; for they know not what they do.'††† But He *chose* to die for His friends, for all of His followers. That was the greatest single act of love which man has ever seen."

Isaac was silent again, staring straight ahead.

***John 4:22
†††Luke 23:34

163

Then he asked, "If I look out at the water, will I see Him walking on it?"

Joshua hesitated. Then he said, "You'll see Him wherever you look."

Isaac looked at the sea, trying to see Jesus. Joshua bowed his head in prayer. Some ten minutes passed very slowly.

Finally Isaac said, "I do see Him."

Joshua wasn't aware of Isaac's meaning. Did he really see Jesus out there on the sea? Joshua would not have been surprised if that was what Isaac meant. Or did he "see" the Lord intellectually? Had he finally come to see the truth? Joshua well knew, in his particular ministry, that the Jewish people required a sign, and he knew further that they sometimes actually got one. How benevolent the Lord was with His own. They were spiritually blind; but Jesus had healed the blind in His earthly ministry, and He continued in that office even now. The little miracle of the wedding story might have been sign enough for Isaac, a sensitive, spiritual personality. But in any case, he had now seen the Lord. Joshua's heart was joyful.

"Do you believe in Jesus?" he asked Isaac.

"Yes," Isaac said decisively. "I believe in Him. He is my Messiah."

"Praise God," Joshua breathed.

Another silence of some minutes occurred as Isaac sat with his eyes closed. Joshua did not attempt to break into his thoughts at such a moment but instead talked with God in his own heart. How good it was to see one of the Lord's own brothers saved! How glorious a moment it was to see a man's heart change. How wonderful to know that Isaac's entire life was now going to take a new direction, and that he was rapidly going to become God's true servant. Joshua was deeply thankful to God.

Joshua saw that Isaac's face was wet with tears as he looked at the sea again. He seemed to shiver once, getting control of his feelings. Then he looked at Joshua with a smile. "Do I have to become a missionary now?" he asked.

"God will tell you what to become from here on." Joshua smiled back.

"Joshua, I'm filled with—some kind of wonder. I feel different—I don't feel like me!"

"Well, you're not the *old* you anymore, that much I can tell you. You're a new person—born again. I felt wonderful when I met the Lord. I know just how you feel."

Suddenly Isaac fell into Joshua's arms, saying, "Dear brother, dear brother!" They held each other for a moment before Isaac said quietly, "Praise God!"

Joshua asked, "Will you pray with me now, Isaac?"

"Of course I will."

They broke their embrace and each bowed his head, but Joshua found it difficult to word his prayer. There was a long pause until he finally said in a hoarse voice, "Thank You, Father. In Jesus' precious name, *thank You!*"

Isaac was smiling at him as he looked up. "Please continue to pray for me now, dear brother. I think I'm going to need your prayers."

Neither man had mentioned Rebecca during their talk, but neither had forgotten her. They knew she was waiting at the kibbutz, perhaps expecting the imminent appearance of her bridegroom. But now things had taken quite a change. Isaac brought it up first.

"You know that Rebecca is waiting."

"I know."

"What now?"

Joshua smiled at him again, indicating that he foresaw no real problem. "God is in charge of your affairs now, Isaac, and God will not have you marry a woman who does not follow the Messiah. God will act to correct this situation."

Looking at Joshua cautiously, Isaac told him firmly, "I'm going to marry Rebecca, Joshua. I haven't changed my mind about *that!* She will surely see what I have seen, in time, but I love her and I have made my promise to her."

Joshua was laughing. "Please, brother, don't accuse me of canceling your wedding plans! It's just that I know God will work this out. As I know Him, He will remedy the situation. Rebecca will be a believer before you marry her. God is not going to forget Rebecca, believe me."

"But I want to marry her *now*. She's there waiting. I want to go and get her immediately!"

"Well, I surely don't blame you," Joshua exclaimed cheerily. "I would want to do the same thing. There never was a bridegroom who was not in a hurry! But, Isaac, I want to do you one more service, if you'll let me. And it's thoroughly biblical. Let me go and get your bride for you."

"*You!*" Isaac exclaimed incredulously. "The *bridegroom* is supposed to get the bride. How is your idea biblical? And why do you want to do it, anyway?"

Joshua was pleased with the situation. He had seen what was developing from the beginning and now he was more than ready to participate in what he perceived to be a lovely miracle. He explained his perceptions to Isaac. "Brother Isaac, we're the main characters in one of those repeat performances by God. Think about your name and your heritage. The Bible says in Genesis 24 that when Isaac was to have a wife, a servant was sent to get her for him. The servant was like the Holy Spirit; he brought the things of the bridegroom to the bride, and he brought the bride back with him. The servant traveled to where Rebekah was, and 'Rebekah came out, who was born to Bethual.'[†††] And he brought her back, and Isaac went out to meet her, just as the Messiah will come on the clouds to meet all of the believers, *His* Bride. I'll go to Rebecca for you, and I'll tell her what has happened to you here. Just as the servant brought gifts to Isaac's

††† Genesis 24:15

167

bride, I'll bring her the greatest gift you possess. I'll tell her that you believe in the Messiah, and I *know* God will open her heart to that. If I have to testify to her all night, I'll bring her back to you a believer! I know Rebecca and I know the Messiah. Believe me, they want to meet each other!"

Isaac was dumbfounded. "This is incredible," he finally blurted out, shaking his head. "It would be wonderful if she would believe you. But how can you be so confident?"

"Rebekah in the Bible never even saw her bridegroom, and yet she came, believing what the servant told her. *Your* Rebecca already loves you. And if you'll trust God and pray with me as I go, I feel sure I'll bring you back your bride. Will you trust the Messiah that far? Will you believe He can do this?"

What could Isaac say? His revelation of only a few minutes before had caused him to completely trust the Messiah. If the Jewish Messiah couldn't be trusted, who could? And yet, this was a vital, earthly matter. Rebecca was a willful woman who knew her own heart. He had to confess to a little doubt in his heart. "What about her father?" he finally asked. "What is *he* going to think of all this, even if she *does* come with you?"

"You're doing what he asked, Isaac. He wanted you to fulfill the wedding custom, and you couldn't possibly do it better. As I understand Rabbi Bethuel, he will have enough knowledge of God to realize that all this is valid. His choice regarding the Messiah is his own affair; we only testify. But a man of his knowledge and love cannot refuse to listen in a spiritual situation like this. When you and Rebecca go to him, you'll have his blessings, I feel sure."

Isaac was amazed at Joshua's confidence, but somehow he was also swept along with it. It would certainly be a miracle if it all happened somehow, but Isaac was inclined to try it. He voiced aloud, "It would be a miracle."

"I'm a Christian; I love with miracles every day," Joshua answered. Then he said, "Pray with me now."

The two men bowed their heads together, asking Godspeed for Joshua's unique mission. For the missionary, it was a calling more precious and vital than any he had ever undertaken. For Isaac, it would be the fulfillment of his fondest dreams. If only Rebecca would come to him with Joshua, everything would work out, he felt. He confined his earnest prayer to the salvation of his bride.

ELEVEN

After her bath, Rebecca put on traveling clothes. She just couldn't help it.

It was dark now and she really should have put on her nightgown and gone to bed. But, she thought, if she was supposed to be waiting to go with her bridegroom, then she had better stay dressed, at least until midnight.

Somehow she had become anxious and nervous throughout the evening, and very aware that her night might be this night. Nothing prevented Isaac from coming immediately, she had been thinking, and her intuition had been nagging her for hours.

She had fashioned a veil from a scarf and placed it with her flashlight by the door. She couldn't resist testing the flashlight once more. As she did, she saw that it burned brightly—still full of "oil." If she heard any noise outside, she could have her veil on and her flashlight in hand in a moment. And after all, she was supposed to have a moment to be ready—Isaac was supposed to shout outside her door. (In reality, she hoped he wouldn't shout very loud. A real shout would bring some uninvited wedding guests immediately; the kibbutz sentries would be there in force in seconds!)

She had packed for an extended trip—at least seven days according to tradition—and had placed her bag by the door. Then she began to pace, feeling the jumpy eagerness of centuries of Jewish brides who had put in their waiting time nightly. No wonder Jewish marriages were sound; the wedding itself came as such a relief! After a whole year of such pacing and waiting, the bride must have been more than ready to marry!

She assumed, of course, that Isaac had planned ahead for a rabbi to marry them after he "abducted" her, and she was curious to see where he would find one who would stay up so late. She certainly was not going on her honeymoon without a legal wedding service, tradition or no tradition, but she would trust Isaac to think of that.

Her thoughts began to blur, and she became very tired. It certainly had been a long, confusing day. She sat wearily in a stuffed chair near the door, and concentrating on being alert to the slightest sound outside she dozed off with a smile on her beautiful face.

At that moment Joshua was making his way into the kibbutz on his hands and knees.

In his spiritual reverie, the overwhelmed Isaac had not thought of all the details, but Joshua had known as he set out that this could be a dangerous mission. For one thing, he could be shot sneaking around the kibbutz after dark. Or he could be peacefully apprehended, but then he would certainly have to make another trip downtown to talk with Inspector Cohen. Such a bizarre circumstance would undoubtedly reopen the inspector's investigation, and Joshua would have a hard time explaining this incredible mission of evangelism.

God had never called him to anything more difficult. But then, witnessing to the Jews was always a challenge of one kind or another. He had protected young Jewish Christians from their own offended families on many occasions; he had witnessed to Arabs in plain sight of tough Jewish soldiers and policemen; and he had approached a rabbi of very Orthodox ways and brought him to the Messiah. But this mission probably took the prize. Never had he been called to penetrate the borders of a northern kibbutz, let alone one which had seen an invasion that very week! He had to be careful, and in constant prayer. *God, help me help the Jews* had been his lifelong prayer, and he uttered it repeatedly now.

And then there was Rebecca. He was nearly as afraid of *her* reaction as he was of the sentries'. For Isaac's sake, he prayed that her heart would be open, and he still felt confident of it. But it was possible that she wouldn't even give him a hearing. He anticipated much less difficulty getting *out* of the kibbutz, accompanied by

Rebecca, though it would be better if they were not seen at all. But would she really come?

She *had* to come. This was a big moment of Isaac's life. With God's help, he just had to persuade her.

Isaac lay on his back in the grass on the hill by the sea, contemplating the stars. It was a beautiful, balmy night, warm with a slight breeze from the water, and Isaac felt very peaceful. Considering the circumstances, he was one of the most peaceful men on the earth at that moment.

He had been talking with God on and off, and he was no more confident that Rebecca would return soon with Joshua. Hours might pass until the two of them made their way back, but Isaac felt that Joshua would succeed in bringing her both to the Lord and to her husband. Joshua could do the impossible.

Lying there, he had offered a prayer for Rebecca—that God might reach out to her and that her heart might be open—and he could only conclude that his prayer would be answered. Joshua was so confident, and surely, as the missionary had said, God wouldn't want him to marry a woman who did not follow the Messiah.

Rebecca heard the footsteps as she slept in her chair, and they disturbed her. Her eyes opened with the knowledge that something was wrong. Somehow she realized immediately that it was not Isaac who was approaching the door.

Although she was not quite fully awake and aware of her circumstances, her hand moved reflexively toward her machine gun. These days, she felt terrorists approaching even in her dreams. She sat perfectly still, listening.

In another moment she heard a familiar voice. "Rebecca," came the whisper outside the door, and she recognized Joshua's voice. She smiled immediately, assuming that Isaac would be with him. This was her wedding party, come to take her off!

At that moment she felt very much indeed like a woman. She felt as the brides of the ancient days must have felt as they were about to commit themselves completely to their chosen men. She felt a strange yearning for Isaac's strong arms; he had not touched her except for the embraces in the nursery on the morning of the terrorist attack, but suddenly her mind was full of those embraces. She got up eagerly and went to the door, with a quick glance at her evil and her flashlight. Opening the door a crack, she looked into the warm and friendly face of Joshua. Immediately she asked, "Is anyone with you?" in a very mischievous voice.

"Rebecca, I'm alone," Joshua whispered. "Please let me in quickly."

Rebecca opened the door, completely shattered. What had gone wrong? This was a strange way to abduct the bride!

Joshua hurried in, with a glance behind him into the darkness. Rebecca closed the door, and he relaxed. Rebecca looked at her visitor in confusion.

"Please sit down," Joshua said, gesturing to her chair. "I have to tell you something."

"Where is Isaac?" she demanded, beginning to feel afraid. "What has happened to him?"

"Rebecca," he began, but she interrupted immediately.

"Has something happened to Isaac?" she hissed.

"No, no. He's fine. Nothing is wrong. Please be calm. That's not it."

Rebecca sat down, feeling relieved, but eyed her visitor warily. She said quietly, "I'm glad to see you, Joshua, but I don't know why you've come."

"Isaac and I had a long talk today," he began, trying to make his voice casual. But Rebecca's eyes brood through him, trying to read his mind. She stared into his face until he had to stop talking. Suddenly she put her right hand to her throat, as if in fear.

"You converted him to Christianity!" she spat out.

Joshua sat motionless, amazed at her intuition. He couldn't find his voice in the presence of such emotion. Rebecca's look was murderous; she looked as though she wanted to kill him. Finally he said in almost a whisper, "I didn't; God did."

Rebecca's eyes slowly closed, and she sat back in her chair, assimilating the shocking news. She just sat there breathing deeply as Joshua waited for her reaction. His mind said, *Lord, please!*

Rebecca spoke at last. "It's not fair," she said in a dull, flat voice. "I want my man the way he was."

Joshua just waited. He could understand her shock and anger at that moment. She was like many a wife of a Jewish convert, completely stunned by what she regarded as a spiritual tragedy. He said calmly, "Will you listen to me?"

Rebecca was silent, not responding to his question, acting as if he hadn't spoken at all. Was this the end of the interview? Wouldn't she even give him a hearing? Was she going to throw him out? Would she just forget Isaac? Was that what she was working on in this awful silence? He had to get her out of that chair.

"Rebecca, I've come a long way, and it's very hot. Could I have some water?"

She opened her eyes, looking away from him, and got up automatically. She went into the next room and appeared a moment later with a glass of water. She handed it to him and sat back down listlessly.

Joshua drank the whole glass of water quickly, and as he did so he had a sudden inspiration. He began to speak, completely unaware that he could quote from memory the biblical passage that came out of his mouth at that nervous moment. " 'And the damsel was very fair to look upon.' " He began, as Rebecca looked at him strangely, " 'a virgin, neither had any man known her: and she went down to the well, and filled her pitcher, and came up. And the servant ran to meet her, and said, Let me, I pray thee, drink a little water of thy pitcher.' "*

Rebecca interrupted and finished the Scripture for him, whispering, " 'And she said, Drink, my lord.' "†

"You know the passage," Joshua observed.

"I once memorized Genesis 24," Rebecca said, still wary of Joshua. "It's about Rebekah, after all. It was my favorite chapter of the Scriptures."

For a moment, they were both avoiding further conversation about the situation with Isaac. Rebecca obviously wanted to hear more, but she was loathe to help Joshua with his message. She was the same as Isaac, though Joshua, when Isaac had said "No Jesus!"

"Did you know that Jesus once asked a woman for water at a well in Samaria?" Joshua asked her.

"No, I didn't know that," she replied coldly.

"As it turned out, He was the one who had the water. Living water." Joshua stopped as he saw a tear start down Rebecca's cheek.

At that very moment, a retired naval officer named Solomon, dozing in the sentry quarters at the main gate, heard his walkie-talkie beep. The walkie-talkie was in his lap as he sat back in a titled chair in front of an electric board resembling a telephone switchboard. As he came instantly awake, he noted the small red light

*Genesis 24:16–17
†Genesis 24:18

glowing in the portion of the kibbutz map on the wall in the sector code-named Zion. His switchboard was lit in the corresponding spot.

"Go ahead, Zion," he said quickly, trying to remain calm. It was Solomon's assignment to monitor the call of all the border sentries of the kibbutz through the night.

"We have penetration in Zion sector," said a tense voice. Solomon recognized the voice of his partner, Lev, with whom he usually patrolled the kibbutz perimeter in the darkness.

"How many men, Lev?" he asked, talking very fast as he reached for the row of buttons at the base of the board.

"It's just a narrow channel through the powder line. Maybe an animal, maybe one man crawling," the walkie-talkie crackled.

Solomon shook his head, trying to think clearly. One man crawling? Why Zion sector? It was mostly dorms, heavily patrolled. His fingers nervously passed back and forth over the Alert buttons. With one of them he could light Zion sector with powerful searchlights and set off screaming alarms. With another he could light the entire kibbutz and also signal the border army base and the Tiberias police. A third button which had to be operated in conjunction with another officer at another board, would ring an alarm at the high command in Jerusalem.

Maybe it was just a small animal that had wandered over the kibbutz powder line and disturbed the surface. Men usually *ran* over the line, unaware of the dust surface in the dark until they had passed over it. Then, unless they realized what they had done and took costly time to cover their tracks, their presence was certain to be detected.

Most of the kibbutz was asleep; very few lights were left on. Solomon hesitated another moment, deciding whether to hit the Zion Alert button, which would bring one hundred armed men out of their beds in a matter of ten or fifteen seconds He himself had only three seconds to reach the decision.

"Sector search, thirty-thirty," he said into his walkie-talkie, in the peculiar, emotionless voice meant to keep everyone calm during such crises. Lev would deploy men to thoroughly search Zion sector in response to this order, and he would report to Solomon every thirty seconds until they found something. If he failed to report at any thirty-second interval, Solomon would use his Alert buttons; the kibbutz would be at full battle trim, with every square foot covered in less than one minute.

In Zion sector, men began to move about like shadows in the night as Joshua and Rebecca continued their crucial conversation.

Rebecca recovered herself in a moment and wiped away the single tear that had betrayed her disappointment. But now she could not maintain the decisive manner she had taken with Joshua. Her feelings wanted to pour forth, and she had difficulty talking. She hoped she wouldn't cry again.

"Does he still want me?" was all she could ask.

"Of course he does," Joshua assured her. "More than ever."

"Then why didn't he come for me?" she demanded, her voice quivering.

"I think he wanted you to talk to me first, Rebecca," Joshua told her as gently as he could. "His new beliefs are very important to him."

She shook her head in confusion, and her eyes became wet again. "I want to see him," she said, half weeping. "I want to talk to him."

At that moment Rebecca perceived a figure moving in the darkness through curtained window behind Joshua. She immediately realized that his entry to the kibbutz had been detected. "Joshua, we can't get out now. The sentries will stop us. Oh, why didn't Isaac come?"

Joshua glanced at the window; he had been aware of this possibility from the beginning. "How long will they search?" he asked, knowing that Rebecca knew the security procedures.

"No one can go outside for a least an hour." Then she gave a real sob. "I couldn't get married if I wanted to now!"

Joshua waited, hoping there wouldn't be a knock on the door. "Will they come in here?" he asked her.

"No, I could have already touched my alarm

button. They're just searching the grounds."

Joshua realized with appreciation that every room of the kibbutz was wired. Since Rebecca hadn't given the signal, they were temporarily safe.

"They'll search for an hour, and then they'll stop. But they'll be alert for the rest of the night. I don't think you can make it out of the kibbutz."

"I'll make it, and you will, too," Joshua stated firmly. "Because that's God's will!"

"What are you talking about?" she asked derisively.

"Just listen to me!" Joshua said. "I'm losing patience with you!"

It was a surprising tone that he took so suddenly. Rebecca saw that his face was tight and his forehead wet. She reacted with compassion, suddenly seeing that he had indeed gone to a great deal of trouble to come to her. She reached out and touched his arm. "Joshua, you have to stay for an hour, anyway. I'll listen to you. Tell me what happened."

"Rebecca, Rebecca!" he said, his head shaking as he tried to control himself. "How stubborn you are! What a true daughter of Israel you are! Stiff-necked, arrogant—"Suddenly he stopped and took a deep breath. "I have spent my life doing this, Rebecca. Arguing with my own people for *their* own salvation. It's not as if I'm paid for this or that I enjoy it so much, believe me. They practically spit at me in the streets. Do you think I have no feelings? Do you think I like being insulted for my faith?

"Day and night I watch our people suffer, as we have suffered for so long. And I have the solution—*I have the Messiah!* But will anyone appreciate what I have? Do they ever give thanks to God for coming here and being nailed to a cross?

"No, they want to be Jews without meeting any of the requirements for being Jews. They have no Messiah and they have no sacrifices and they have no Temple and they have no faith!"

Rebecca became almost frightened as Joshua poured out all his feelings. Obviously he was tense and scared about all that had happened to him during this long day, and he now had nearly reached his breaking point.

"And for centuries we have been punished—for almost two thousand years we have been punished—for this terrible mistake, for rejecting our loving God and His suffering Messiah, and it still never occurs to any of us, in our magnificent pride, that something is *wrong!* Well, that's not what God wants! That's not what we were chosen for! We are a long way from God, and we are paying for it, believe me, woman!

"So today is a typical day for me—for a disciple of Jesus Christ! I have to be interrogated by the police of my own nation as though I were a subversive; I have to teach the Bible to a Jew who warns me not to mention the name of his own Messiah; and I have to come out here on my hands and knees, waiting to be shot in the back at any moment, in order to fetch him a wife! Well, I'll tell you something. It may be a terrible sin on my part, but I'm beginning to get *tired* of this!"

He paused for a moment, breathing hard, but Rebecca could say nothing. She was completely transfixed by this bitter speech, and feeling very guilty besides. She sat in silent wonder as Joshua's angry eyes flashed at her.

"Now, you'll sit here and you'll hear the truth for one hour! This is what God has arranged for you, whether you appreciate that or not; and if you want to reject the Messiah, you can do that in an hour. But for now you're going to hear the gospel, even if I have to tie you to that chair!"

There was something very appealing in Joshua's fury. Rebecca sensed that the missionary would rather have done anything in the world than become so frustrated with her, but obviously this gospel meant so much to him that he'd lost his grip. He cared. He cared about her and he cared about Isaac. That he had taken a chance tonight on sudden death was true. That he cared deeply about his people was also true.

"Now, let me start with your wedding ceremony. It's yours, not mine. Your father taught it to you, but he doesn't know its real meaning, and I *do!* The whole thing talks about Christ, just as everything else in Jewish custom and Law talks about Christ. When I explained it to Isaac, he saw the truth, and the truth set him free. He's not engaged just to you now; he's also engaged to

183

the Messiah. And I pray God you'll be saved, too," finished Joshua in a softer voice.

Rebecca caught the tremendous emotion behind Joshua's last statement. Truly it was important to him that Rebecca appreciate the Messiah, at least as Joshua saw the Messiah. She determined to listen with an open mind. Later she would check with Isaac about what he really felt about this whole matter.

Joshua began the gospel in his traditional way: "There was an old covenant, and now there is a new covenant."

TWELVE

It was nearly dawn when Isaac spotted the beam of light coming out of the trees. At first he didn't know if he really saw it or not. He had been sleeping on and off, and gazing at the silvery sea lit by brilliant moonlight.

It seemed to be a flashlight that he saw, cautiously being turned on and off as its carrier came through the brush. Soon he could make out two people, and his heart began to sing! Like Isaac in the Bible, he ran out to meet them.

Rebecca ran ahead of Joshua to fall into Isaac's arms. She was wearing her veil. "My love!" Isaac exulted as he held her.

Joshua stood off to one side, watching the two embrace. Minutes passed as they just held each other.

Finally, at Joshua's suggestion, they made their way down the hill to the water's edge, where they would not be noticeable to passing soldiers or police. Joshua walked apart from the two, letting them talk together privately. He knew they had a great deal to talk about.

As they walked along, Rebecca brought up the

crucial subject. "Darling," she said, "I listened very carefully to what Joshua told me. He said he told you the same things—about the wedding, and—the Messiah."

It was hard for Isaac to have this sort of conversation with a veiled woman, but he had asked her during their first embrace if he might remove it and she said, "Of course not. We're not married yet!" Her impish smile had almost penetrated the veil.

Now he told her firmly, "I believe Joshua, and I believe in the Messiah. It's my wish that you believe the same way."

She walked along in silence, seemingly to contemplate that.

"Rebecca, I love you," Isaac went on as they walked. "I suppose I would marry you no matter what you believed, but it would grieve me if we were so different on such a vital thing. What Joshua told me, right from our own Scriptures is undoubtedly true. Jesus is the Messiah. That's what I believe."

He put his arm around her tightly, trying to encourage her to speak up, but she was silent. He just had to know, and immediately, what she thought about this. "Rebecca —" he began, but she cut him off.

She said pleasantly, "You're walking awfully close for a man on a date with a Christian girl."

At the water's edge they sat down on soft sand, and the three listened to the small waves lapping the shore. Joshua and Rebecca filled Isaac in on the night's difficulties at the kibbutz. Isaac was amazed that they had gotten out at all, and was very apologetic about sending Joshua there without thinking about the possible consequences.

"Well, your mind was a million miles from things like kibbutz security," Joshua told him. "But I was on God's mission, and God was with me. I've had a little bit of combat experience, too."

"What Israeli hasn't?" Isaac said. "But how did you get back out with Rebecca? Didn't they try to stop you?"

Rebecca said, "He just put his arm around me, and we strolled out of the main gate like lovers. I know we were seen, but there are lots of couples walking around on kibbutzim at night. If the terrorists ever figure out that approach, we're in for it."

"Love always works on the Jews," Joshua added significantly.

"Well, surely you didn't wear that veil out of the main gate?" Isaac asked.

"Oh, no." Rebecca laughed. "I just put that on for you. I don't need protection from *them*, I need protection from *you!*"

"Well, for heaven's sake," Isaac exclaimed. "How long are you going to wear that thing?"

"Until you marry me," the lady answered. He couldn't see her smile, of course, but her eyes had that crinkled look that went with her most devastating teasing.

"Well, with everything that has been going on, I didn't think about a wedding. I mean, what do you expect?"

"Perfectly all right," retorted Rebecca. "If the Arab women can wear veils all their lives, I certainly can!" Her eyes were more crinkled than ever.

"Joshua!" Isaac appealed helplessly.

"Never mind," the missionary said, laughing. "Your wedding is the first thing on our agenda. As soon as it gets light, we can walk into town and go to the mission. We have contact with a rabbi who believes in the Messiah. This won't be the first wedding he had performed on short notice. He's accustomed to God's will. If you'd like to stay at the mission a few days before getting married, I'll be glad to go to Jerusalem and talk with your father, Rebecca. Possibly I can get him to come to the wedding, or at least to give his blessing."

Both Isaac and Rebecca were struck by Joshua's endless services and energy. He was like a very old friend, willing to give his all. He would even try to take on Rebecca's recalcitrant father. *And*, Isaac thought, *he certainly can bring him to the Messiah if anyone can!*

But Rebecca spoke first. "I already have my father's blessing to marry Isaac. And besides, you've certainly done enough. I already plan to name our first son Joshua. As to what has happened here spiritually, I can tell you this: my father will not object to this marriage once he meets Isaac and hears our whole story. He is not the kind of man who disowns a child, and he is more tolerant than many people think. I know the man. He'll rejoice with us eventually."

Isaac couldn't help but yawn. It had been a long day and night. He thought about Rabbi Bethuel's request concerning the wedding custom, and asked Joshua, "Is there any way we can reasonably copy the wedding tradition? I'll say this much—I don't want to wait around for Rebecca after all the trouble we've gone to!"

Joshua laughed. "We have a *chuppa*—a canopy—at the mission, and that's what the Jews use these days to symbolize the old bridal chamber. You've certainly made your contract, and you've been apart from your bride about as long as a man like you can stand. We drink the cup at the wedding, so that takes care of that part. As for your honeymoon, it's supposed to be at the home of the bridegroom's father. But why don't you telephone Jerusalem and ask the rabbi if he has room for two? I have a feeling he'll provide a first-class marriage supper for you."

Isaac was delighted, but Rebecca was thinking ahead. Her eyes were dark in concentration for a moment. Then she repeated, "I know the man. Everything will be joyful in the end."

Joshua strolled away to the water's edge. He was smiling. Obviously he had left the two alone purposely.

Isaac looked at his veiled bride-to-be. Her eyes told him of great love. Holding her two hands tightly in his, he closed his eyes and began to pray.

"Dear Lord, thank You for bringing us together and bringing us to You. We pray for all those around us, that they will understand us. help us to have the courage to tell them that we have found *Yeshua HaMaschiach*. Comfort our parents as they encounter this new idea. Let them have Your gifts of peace and understanding. Thank You for Joshua, and for all the miracles You have worked through him. Amen."

Rebecca was silent, her eyes also closed. She held Isaac's hands tightly. She thought about how they must look to God, standing there together by the sea. As she opened her eyes, she realized that the sky had brightened and that the sun was about to rise. The water sparkled, and birds were singing on all sides of them. She looked at Isaac but his eyes remained closed.

Then she drew her hands back and lifted her veil. As Isaac's eyes opened, he saw her face very close to his. It was beautiful. Her eyes were glowing, her lips soft and smiling slightly. She kissed him lightly on the mouth and then whispered, "The next kiss will be under the canopy. Now come along, my love, and marry me." And she quickly replaced the veil.

The three of them walked away from the water's edge just as the sun rose over the sea.

Made in the USA
Middletown, DE
23 November 2022

15234251R00106